COURTSHIPS

D0887966

Courtships

N.R. KING

LUMINARE PRESS

WWW.LUMINAREPRESS.COM

Cover Design by Claire Flint Last

Luminare Press
442 Charnelton St.
Eugene, OR 97401
www.luminarepress.com

LCCN: 2019905215
ISBN: 978-1-64388-099-0

To Andy

Contents

The Bouquet of Rose Hip Jelly

1932

ADDY LOVED THE TRANQUILITY OF MORNING IN THE kitchen. After her mother and her sister left for the shop, she was free to sip her tea and pretend this was her house and she was its mistress, though, in fact, she had just graduated from school and was only fifteen years old.

With sunshine spreading across the table and a sweet breeze bringing garden fragrances right into the house, this morning was particularly conducive to her fantasies. Addy felt pride in the neat, clean kitchen but imagined it yet more grand, filled with lovely new china in a floral pattern and new dish towels to match. Fortunately, the kitchen was already painted yellow, the only color for a kitchen, so she didn't need to repaint it in her mind.

New colors in the garden, though, would be just the thing. Bright, bold flowers and a new flowering tree would make a splash and set her garden above all the others on the street. Mama and Rose would say they had never known anyone so clever with plants, and the neighbors would exclaim, "What a remarkable garden. We never would have thought to plant such exotic flowers or create so original a setting. Beautiful, quite beautiful, and daring."

Addy was preparing her humble response to their effusive praise when Bess destroyed the illusion by bursting through the back door, her hat uncharacteristically askew and her purse dangling from her arm.

"Mama! What's wrong?" Addy asked, jumping up and trying to guide her mother to a chair. "Why aren't you at the shop with Rose? Is she ill? Are you ill?"

"Enough questions, Addy. Sit down and be quiet. I didn't rush home for conversation. I came to tell you there'll be company for dinner."

Addy sat down as directed. Company? Company was unusual, but company in the middle of the week was unheard of. She knew a burst of inquisitiveness was less likely to be rewarded with information than a show of benign indifference. Addy took a sip of tea.

"Addy, are you listening? I want you to buy a nice brisket and cook it with onions and carrots like I showed you last Friday, and be sure to make a potato kugel. Don't forget gravy for the brisket, and bake challah rolls and an apple cake for dessert."

"Who's coming to dinner? The King? I thought old George was too ill to travel."

"Just do as I say. Have everything ready for dinner at seven. Don't come to the shop this afternoon. Just take care of dinner."

"You haven't told me who's getting the royal treatment."

"A boy I met at the bank this morning. He just arrived here yesterday and was trying to open an account. Poor thing, he didn't even know how to count his money. So I helped him, and we had a lovely chat about how ample the Scottish breakfast is. A big meal in the morning is something new for him. We agreed that neither of us likes orange marmalade, and we wondered why the Scots seem to like it so much. He's a nice boy, and lonely. I knew he would appreciate a touch of home, so I asked him to dinner." Bess opened her purse. "You'll need money for the shopping."

While her mother pulled coins out of her change purse, Addy looked out the window. A boy who doesn't like marmalade...coming to dinner. What sort of a mysterious stranger could this be? She knew her mother wouldn't concern herself with a local Edinburgh boy who couldn't open a bank account, and if he couldn't count the money, he wasn't from England or South Africa. So he was almost certainly a new medical student from America. The best sort of mysterious stranger.

"Addy, pay attention. There's one more thing. Do Rose a favor and iron her new white blouse and her blue skirt so she can change quickly when we get home from the shop." Her mother left a stack of coins on the table and hurried out the back door.

Addy sat at the table. She knew exactly what was on her mother's mind. With just four hundred Jewish families in Edinburgh, the choice of marriageable partners was limited, and her mother was one of many Jewish mothers hoping to marry daughters to Jewish medical students. As a widow, she didn't have the advantage of a husband who could befriend students at synagogue and bring them home for a meal after the service. Now a boy had crossed her path before anybody else had met him. He must seem like a gift from God.

Addy wondered if the incoming students realized the excitement their arrival caused, or the urgency the news from Germany had added to the scheming among the Jewish housewives. The Jewish community often knew more about events in Germany than the newspapers reported, and, although not every report seemed credible, her mother believed them all. She believed that Mrs. Bloomfield's uncle had been dragged from his law office and beaten by police. She believed that Mrs. Eidler's cousins were now shunned in the neighborhood where they had lived for years. She knew that mobs had broken into homes and forced Jews into the street where they were pelted with stones and rocks thrown by jeering teenagers. Only Mrs. Gertenson's brother was not believed when he wrote that if Jews showed themselves to be loyal, upstanding German citizens, this wave of anti-Semitism would pass. Her mother didn't believe that for a minute, and she didn't let her daughters believe it either.

"Your life has been too good," she would tell them, smoothing her hair, and straightening her collar as if readying herself for a journey. "You didn't run from Russia, one step ahead of the mob, carrying a baby in your arms. You have no idea what can happen, and you need to be ready." Though Addy knew all about the troubles in Europe, she couldn't bring herself to brood over people in Germany she hadn't met. Why ruin today?

Addy glanced at the clock as she rinsed her teacup in the sink. Hitler won't knock on the door anytime soon, but the boy will be here in a few hours. She licked the tip of her pencil just like her mother always told her not to, and sat at the table to make a shopping list. Since apples from the tree in the garden were better for eating than for baking this time of year, she put apples on her list, and brisket. She had enough onions, but she added carrots and doodled a little bouquet of flowers at the bottom of the paper. Things certainly change in an instant, she thought.

Mama must be hoping he'll marry Rose, even though Rose is older than the first-year students by four years and probably smarter than most of them. But, even though I'm not quite five years younger than the new students, maybe he'll want a younger girl, a prettier girl. She added ribbons with long streamers to her doodle until it became a bridal bouquet.

Addy got her hat and coat and stuffed the shopping list into her pocket. She would need to hurry in order to get an

N.R. King

early start on dinner and have plenty of time to iron Rose's outfit as well as her own mauve dress with the lace collar.

AN HOUR LATER, ADDY RETURNED AND SET OUT HER PUR-chases on the kitchen table. She smiled as she unwrapped the brisket. Old Mr. Baum, the butcher, had held up a three-pound brisket for her to see before he wrapped it saying, "Here's just the brisket for your family."

Not today, Addy thought. Boys have big appetites. "I'll need a six-pound brisket, please," she said.

"Now, why are you needing a six-pound brisket in the middle of the week?"

Addy stared at him. He would never dare ask her mother such a question. She drew herself up, preparing an answer to such impertinent curiosity when she heard the door open behind her.

"Good morning, Mrs. Tendler," Mr. Baum said.

"Good morning, Mr. Baum, and good morning to you, as well, Addy." Mrs. Tendler approached the counter and smiled at Addy. "Please tell your mother how much I like the black gloves I bought from her last week."

"Mother will be pleased to hear that you are happy with them."

Mr. Baum winked as he handed Addy her package, and she reluctantly swallowed the biting retort she had prepared for him. It's a pity I can't ask if he demands an accounting of how the meat's to be used from all his customers. But it would never do to appear impolite in front of Mrs. Tendler.

The best Addy could do was nod and leave with what she hoped was an air of mystery. She had to be content that Mr. Baum's curiosity was not satisfied. And if Mr. Baum and Mrs.

Tendler were left speculating about why she needed such a large brisket, then so much the better. Let them know that her family had its secrets, too.

Addy felt confident in the kitchen. She loved the combination of precision and flair that went into producing a lovely meal, especially for important occasions like tonight. Of course, her mother always took credit for Addy's success, and it was true that when they cooked together, she stood at her mother's elbow and tasted as they went along so she would know what directions like "add sugar till it's sweet enough" meant. Addy was soon devising embellishments to recipes she found in cookbooks, though she never changed any of her mother's recipes. It irked her that tonight's recipes were all from her mother.

After preparing the dough for the challah rolls, Addy took her mother's apple cake recipe from the box kept on the kitchen window ledge, propped it against her tea cup, and began to peel the apples, eating most of the peelings as she went along. They're the best part of the apple, she thought. Why do most people toss them out? After carefully measuring and mixing the ingredients, Addy poured the batter into a cake pan.

The apple doesn't fall far from the tree. That's what her mother said whenever Addy did anything that reminded her of herself, and Addy couldn't keep the phrase from coming to mind as she wiped the batter from the edge of the pan with the same quick, impatient gesture her mother would have used. When she was much younger, Addy used to lie in bed at night and think about a little apple growing at the top of the tree, a magic apple with wings. When it was ripe, it would fly up to the sky instead of falling to the ground. That way it might end up far from the tree, in spite of what her mother said. Addy didn't believe in magic apples anymore, and whenever she found herself doing something her mother would have done, like using the corner of the dishtowel to wipe the edge of a cake pan, she remembered her mother's favorite saying and worried that her mother might be right.

At the first lull in the dinner preparations, Addy turned her attention to setting the table. She had read once in a cookbook that a diner eats first with his eyes. After that, Addy was careful to set a dinner table that announced her competence and good taste, no matter how mundane the meal. She always used a fresh tablecloth with napkins to match, and sometimes she added one flower from the garden in a small vase. She never used a dish or cup that was chipped. They might be fine for breakfast or lunch, but not for dinner. If the next knock on the door was Prince Charming or Elijah the Prophet, she wanted to be prepared to invite him in for a lovely meal.

Now she chose an embossed linen tablecloth and napkins and the silver napkin rings. Let the boy think they dined in such splendor every night. Addy was sure that her mother didn't intend him to join them for a meal around the kitchen table. She set out the white dishes with the gold border and the good silverware and thought about flowers. She had time to cut flowers if she hurried. A moment later, Addy returned from the garden with a handful of pink and white blossoms and tucked them into a small vase. Her mother didn't like to have large vases or tall flowers getting in the way at dinner. Addy set the flowers in the middle of the table and stood back to admire the effect.

The table looked lovely, but in the next instant, Addy reconsidered. If a boy is coming to dinner, he should put flowers on the table. This will be his first test as a suitor. If he doesn't bring flowers, he'll suit Rose just fine. If he brings flowers, he'll be the perfect boy for me. She carried the vase to the front door and placed it on the little shelf under the mirror. Now they would greet the boy as soon as he came into the house.

Even though she understood the importance of a pretty table, Addy thought the cookbook was wrong. She believed that the diner eats first with his nose, and she loved the way the house filled with a rich blend of aromas as she prepared a meal. She wanted everybody who came in the door to savor the fragrance and long for a taste of whatever was cooking in the kitchen. Sometimes Rose would come in after a day at the shop, go directly to the kitchen, and use the big ladle to taste the soup right out of the pot. She would laugh and say, "Delicious, Addy. It's what I've been dreaming of all day."

When the food was cooking nicely and Rose's freshly ironed outfit hung in her closet, Addy ironed her own dress. Rose's simple outfit hadn't required any special care. Just like Rose, herself, Addy thought, while my dress needs an expert touch. So she took her time, even though it was close to six and she wanted to be dressed and in the kitchen when her mother and her sister came home. Addy knew they would go straight to their bedrooms to change, and she wouldn't see them until after the boy arrived. She didn't want her mother to have an opportunity to comment on the fact that she was wearing her new dress, and she was sure that her mother wouldn't say anything in front of the boy. After he was safely in the house, she planned to appear from the kitchen wearing a clean apron so he would know who had prepared the meal. Then she would take off her apron to reveal her new dress. She could imagine the look of admiration on his face when he realized that this lovely girl had produced the delicious meal he was about to enjoy. He would wonder how she managed to look so serene after a day in the kitchen.

Addy dressed quickly, brushed her hair, and added a touch of English lavender on her wrists and behind her ears. She was pleased with her reflection in the mirror. Her brown hair and dark eyes looked good with the mauve dress. And the dress clung where it should and flared where it should. Perfect. It didn't hurt that this boy would be meeting Rose and her at the same time. Addy was a little ashamed at how much she liked being compared to Rose. She knew that their physical contrast favored her. Rose might be the smart daughter, but Addy knew she was the pretty one.

Addy hurried to the kitchen, put on an apron, and turned her attention to the last-minute preparations. Dinner was almost ready when Bess and Rose came home.

"Addy," her mother ordered as soon as she came in. "Take these flowers away. The vase is too heavy for the shelf, and they're about to spill any minute." Then she and Rose hurried to their rooms to change. Addy could hear the two of them washing up and opening drawers. Bess called out, "Is everything ready, Addy?" and Rose added, "Thanks for ironing my blouse." Addy dutifully collected the flowers from the foyer and put them in her own room as she marveled at how the prospect of meeting a boy energizes tired old females.

Promptly at 7:00, they heard a knock on the front door, and Bess went to answer it. Rose was in the front room; Addy stayed in the kitchen. She could hear her mother say, "Douglas, I'm so glad to see you." Then there was the sound of a male voice, and her mother responded, "For me? Completely unnecessary, you know, but very thoughtful of you."

In the kitchen, Addy liked the sound of that low, bass rumble and imagined the big man necessary to produce such a voice. A tall man, with bright brown eyes and light brown hair. With a smooth cheek and a rosy mouth. A slender waist and a hairy chest. And shoulders so broad and arms so long that she would disappear when he hugged her. Then she stopped right there, because that was much too much already. She thought instead about the gift her mother had accepted. He must have brought flowers. A very good omen.

She could hear her mother introduce Douglas to Rose and Rose's polite greeting, and then her mother saying, "I'll just help Addy with the last-minute preparations."

"He's here," her mother whispered as she came into the kitchen.

"I gathered as much," Addy replied and wondered what her mother had done with the bouquet.

"He brought this," her mother said and held out a jar of rose hip jelly. "He must have thought we'd like some variety with our toast in the morning."

Addy looked at the jar. Roses are flowers, but rose hips are seed pods. There seemed to be no way to give the boy credit for flowers when he brought a jar of jelly. What was he thinking? Maybe he thought flowers would be pushy. Especially since her mother had invited him and he needed something more matronly as a gift. So jelly was a good idea with just a hint of flowers on the label. Could he be that clever?

"Is everything done in here?" her mother asked.

Addy nodded.

"And where did you put those flowers?"

"They're in my room. I'll bring them to the shop tomorrow so you and Rose can enjoy them there."

"No, you won't. Flowers don't belong in the shop. Now get out of that apron."

Whatever you say, Addy thought. I'll leave the flowers in my room and have them all to myself. She took off her apron, and, as she had anticipated, her mother frowned.

"Why did you choose your new dress, Addy? There's no need for you to look so fancy."

N.R. King

"I thought we were trying to make a nice impression."

"It's too late to change now. Just come meet him."

In the front room, Rose was sitting on the sofa laughing at something that had just been said, and a young man sat on a chair facing her.

"Douglas, I'd like you to meet my younger daughter, Addy."

Douglas stood and said, "Very nice to meet you," and remained standing until Addy took a place at the other end of the sofa and her mother made herself comfortable in the big winged chair. His blue eyes caught Addy's eye for just a moment before he turned his full attention to her mother. While he answered questions about his family, Addy tried to understand how this man produced that deep voice.

Douglas was only an inch or two taller than she was, and while she was a little tall for a girl, he was certainly a little short for a man. He had tried to slick down his dark hair, but the curls had sprung back and created a dense cloud around his head. A moustache covered his upper lip in a transparent attempt to add years to his youthful appearance. It didn't work. He looked like a little boy wearing his father's moustache. He spoke with a hesitation, not a stutter exactly, but a slight stammer, and seemed small and insecure except for two things, his deep bass voice and the auburn-colored hair covering the backs of his hands. Addy had never seen anybody like him. She had never heard anybody like him either. The raw American accent and the straightforward comments and delivery were new to her. He seemed at once shy and bold.

Douglas's attention never wavered. He sat forward in his chair and listened closely to every question he was asked before answering each one fully. He paid no attention at all to Addy or Rose, and neither of them joined the conversation.

"Tell me about your mother, Douglas."

"My mother's name is Clara, and she's a wonderful woman. She knew I always wanted to be a doctor, and she's the one who made medical school possible."

"How did she do that?"

"I have two younger brothers and a little sister." Douglas looked at Addy and added, "She's younger than you are."

Addy fingered the lace at her collar and crossed her legs, hoping her face didn't show how displeased she was to be compared to his little sister.

"I've worked since I was seven years old, and even though my family isn't well-off, my mother saved every penny I earned. That's how I had enough money to pay my tuition and one way on the ship. There wasn't much left over, so I'll need a part-time job to help make ends meet."

"What kind of work could you do when you were seven?"

"I was a newsboy, and a good one. I had a corner right by a busy downtown trolley stop where I sold papers every evening. And I wasn't just selling papers. I also had to be sure that nobody took my corner, so I was always defending it from older boys. I was a scrappy little kid." With that Douglas stood up and called out, "GET YOUR PAPER HERE! READ ALL ABOUT IT! NEW MEDICAL STUDENT INVITED TO DINNER HIS SECOND NIGHT IN EDINBURGH!" They all laughed. "You would buy a paper with a story like that, wouldn't you, Mrs. Kaminsky?" he asked.

"I would, indeed," she said, and laughed again. "It's nice to hear a happy headline, for a change." There was a moment of silence as she smoothed her hair and straightened the collar of her blouse. When she finally said, "Let's go into the dining room," Addy breathed a sigh of relief. There would be no recitation of the horrors of the Nazis tonight, at least.

"Gosh, this table looks pretty," Douglas said as he sat down across from Addy and Rose.

He seemed surprised when Addy replied, "Thank you," and she realized that he must have meant the compliment for her mother. Wait till dinner, she thought. You'll be amazed.

Rose followed Addy into the kitchen until her mother called to her.

"Rose, come back out here and help me entertain our guest. Addy can manage without you."

Rose looked at Addy and shrugged before returning to the dining room. She's right, Addy thought. No sense in arguing. Our roles are assigned, and we're expected to play our parts.

Addy carried out the brisket in its pan and the gravy boat and went back for a basket of rolls and the potato kugel on a white plate. Finally, she brought the bowl of cooked carrots and a crystal pitcher of cold water to the table. The family didn't usually say a prayer before eating, and there was a moment of hesitation to see if Douglas wanted to say the traditional blessing. When he showed no such inclination, they began passing the serving dishes around the table and helping themselves to the food.

Addy couldn't imagine a more successful meal. The brisket was tender and juicy, the gravy was smooth and luscious, the kugel was high and fluffy, and the carrots were sweet and just a little crunchy. She was proud, and Douglas was effusive in his praise.

"I wondered what smelled so good when I walked in the front door. I had heard that Brits are terrible cooks, but everything here is delicious."

Addy smiled and so did her mother.

"These recipes are from my mother's kitchen in Russia," Bess said. "I wrote them out in detail, and if Addy follows them closely when she cooks, the meals turn out well."

Addy forced herself to concentrate on her plate as her mother stole the compliment about the dinner while describing her as someone who could follow directions.

When Douglas asked about the shop, her mother smoothed her hair and launched into the story of how she and her husband had carried their baby, Rose, in their arms and fled Russia, one step ahead of the pogrom. "We were on our way to the United States, but we ran out of money and settled in Edinburgh. At first, Joseph went door-to-door carrying a pack filled with needles and thread and ribbons and buttons, but, at last, we were able to open our own shop. It's as lovely a place now as it was on our first day. We sell everything a lady needs to dress well and only the best. You'll not find anything second-rate on our shelves. Before he passed away, Joseph said, 'Bess, be sure to keep the shop.' I did just as he asked, and now Rose and I run the business."

"That's an amazing story," Douglas said.

Amazing is right, Addy thought, knowing that it couldn't have happened the way her mother told it. For one thing, Rose was four years old at the time they left Russia, hardly the babe in arms her mother described. So how much was true, and how much was exaggeration? She used to hope that Rose would tell her what had really happened, but whenever Addy asked, Rose insisted that she had no memory of it. It made Addy angry that the rest of the family had shared their most dramatic adventure before she was born and were hiding the story from her.

"The two of us enjoy working in the shop," her mother continued. "But it's Rose that has the good head for business."

Now Douglas turned his attention to Rose. "I admire businesswomen. It's not easy to make your living by convincing other people to want what you have for sale."

N.R. King

Rose smiled. "It's not as hard as you might think," she said. "I try to have the things they want anyway, and then I add a nice little chat to every sale. People like to be listened to, and I like to listen to people. I'd have a hard time as a newsboy because I would want to talk with every customer."

Douglas laughed, and so did Rose. Her big laugh showed her uneven teeth, and as she laughed, one of her hairpins escaped and fell onto the table. She laughed again when she noticed and carelessly stuck it back in her hair.

Addy marveled at her sister's abundant good humor and lack of good sense. If that was me, she thought, I would hide my teeth and secure my hair. But Rose is treating Douglas as an equal or a little brother without thinking about the reasons Mama brought him home. Addy was amazed, and a little grateful. Here was another way the contrast between her and Rose favored her.

"The shop's a great success, Douglas," her mother added quickly, "and it's all Rose's doing. Don't let her humility fool you." She smiled at Rose while Addy scowled at her food. So now their little shop rivals Jenners on Princes Street because Rose is a genius, and dinner is a success because the recipes were perfect.

Douglas helped himself to another portion of everything, and the women took small portions, themselves, so he wouldn't be left eating alone. They dawdled with their food until Douglas declared himself too full to eat another mouthful. When Addy and Rose got up to clear the table, he also stood.

"I can't cook," he said, "but I can carry dishes." Lifting the water pitcher in one hand and the bowl of carrots in the other, he turned toward the kitchen.

"No," Bess said. "You're our guest. Rose, you stay at the table, too. Addy, take those things from Douglas and finish clearing."

Addy reached for the pitcher, but before she had it firmly in her grasp, Douglas let go and the pitcher tipped. Everyone jumped back from the table as water cascaded over the edge and onto the floor.

"Addy, try to pay attention to what you're doing," Bess said. "Go get a towel and wipe this up."

"Let me help," Rose said and began removing the rest of the dishes from the table.

Douglas folded up the edges of the tablecloth. "This is all my fault, not Addy's. Apparently, I can't even carry dishes."

Addy went to the kitchen, replaying Douglas's defense in her mind until it eclipsed her mother's rebuke. By the time she returned with several towels, he had finished folding the tablecloth and was ready to carry the soggy mass to the kitchen.

"Just put it in the sink," Addy said. "I'll tend to it later."

Douglas insisted on helping Rose and Addy wipe up the remaining water. "I'm really sorry for ruining your beautiful table."

"There's no harm done," Addy answered with a smile just for him before she realized that he wasn't looking at her. He was talking to her mother.

"It's only water, Douglas." Bess said. "You were kind to help clean up."

With the table reset for dessert, Bess sent Addy to prepare the tea and serve the cake. When the tea was nicely steeped, Addy carried the teapot to the dining room, where her mother would pour, and returned to the kitchen for the apple cake. She picked it up, hesitated, and put it back on the kitchen table. Why not? A lovely dusting of sugar is just what this cake needs. Not that it's called for in the sacred recipe. Addy grabbed the small sifter and the confectioner's sugar from the pantry shelf. She held her apron over her dress before adding her final touch to the cake and carrying it to the dining room.

Addy was sure she heard Rose gasp when she saw the cake, and Douglas said, "Wow! That's a pretty cake." Her mother had no audible reaction, but she smiled a tight, little smile as she handed Addy a cup of tea.

After the apple cake and tea had been served, Douglas asked Bess if she knew of any rooms for rent. "Right now, I'm staying with another medical student, but I can only impose on him for a short time until I find something for myself."

"I'll ask around," Bess said.

"Could I stop by the shop in a few days? Maybe by then I'll need a button or some thread, and maybe you will have heard of a room for me."

They lingered over their tea until Douglas said that he had to be going. As soon as the door closed behind him, their mother said. "What do you think? I think he's a very nice boy, and I like him." Addy and Rose agreed that he was nice and began to clear the dishes. "Just soak the dishes tonight, Addy. It's late, and you'll keep me awake with your noise in the kitchen. You can clean up in the morning." Her mother paused, "Dinner came out well, Addy, but you need a lesson in carrying water pitchers, and the cake was too sweet."

"Do you want help with the dishes tonight, Addy?" Rose asked after their mother had closed her bedroom door. "I'm not too tired to help you now."

"No thanks. They can wait till morning. You go up to bed." It was late, and Addy knew Rose looked forward to reading before going to sleep. Sometimes her light would still be visible under her door when Addy was ready to turn off her own light, even though Rose might have gone upstairs long before her.

Addy covered her new dress with an apron and turned to the sink. The quiet of the kitchen after dinner was usually a moment she enjoyed as much as she enjoyed the bustle in the kitchen before. But now, the sight of the soggy tablecloth reminded her that Douglas had not said one word directly to her all evening except to compare her to his little sister.

Addy carried the tablecloth to the laundry room and then, very quietly, washed and dried the dinner dishes and set the kitchen table for breakfast. As she worked, she wondered if Douglas would want to marry Rose. Or Rose would want to marry him.

In all her years of working in the shop, Rose had never had a serious beau, and she didn't seem to care. She didn't care about going to dances or meeting boys; she didn't flirt and she didn't agree with a boy just to be agreeable. Once when Addy had tried to commiserate with Rose about all the time and energy the shop took, Rose had looked at her in surprise.

"Don't you know that I love the shop?" she had said. "I love figuring out what will sell and then deciding how much to buy. I love meeting with wholesalers and creating displays, and dealing with customers. The shop is an exciting place. It was like Papa's third child, and I feel that way about it, too."

Addy's perplexed look of disbelief had made Rose laugh. "I can see you find that hard to understand, Addy, but it's true. When I walk into the shop in the morning and the polished wooden counter and the gleaming glass cases welcome me, it's like coming home. The spools of colorful ribbon, the baskets of buttons, and the shelves filled with gloves and scarves and shirts are beautiful. And the back room with its boxes of new items and my work table and my smock hanging in its hook is the coziest room I know. Even with the mop and bucket in the corner," she had added with a smile.

Addy had looked away in embarrassment, and Rose had tried again. "Think of it like this. My feelings about the shop are a bit like your feelings about the garden."

Then Addy appreciated a little of what Rose was trying to explain. The garden was a special place. But she still didn't understand how anybody could compare their beautiful backyard garden filled with fragrances and flowers to the dark, cramped shop stuffed with merchandise.

Maybe it's more like my attachment to the kitchen, she thought. Even when I'm hot and exhausted, I love it anyway, and everybody who comes in seems like my guest. Could that be how Rose feels about customers in the shop? I wonder if Douglas will be as interesting to her.

Addy knew it would be more than three years before her mother would permit her to go to dances or meet medical students. But, perhaps, meeting boys didn't include Douglas. Tonight, he had defended her and helped clean up the spilled water. Maybe next year he would be standing here in her kitchen, drying the dishes as she washed them and kissing her on the cheek and telling her how pretty she is. And her mother would say, "But she's so young," and Douglas would answer, "Love has no age." Addy giggled, very quietly, and hung up the dishtowel. Whatever she did, she knew she would have to be careful not to hurt Rose's feelings, and she'd have to get Douglas to stop comparing her to his little sister.

Addy took one last look at the kitchen table, added the jar of rose hip jelly to the choices already there, and went upstairs.

THE NEXT MORNING, BESS CAME INTO THE KITCHEN FIRST, her flannel robe hastily thrown over her nightie and her hair hanging down her back in a long, thin braid. She was pleased to see that Addy had done the dinner dishes and set the table for breakfast. That child's just like me, she thought, as she emptied the kettle, filled it with fresh water, and set it on the burner to boil. Then she noticed the jar of rose hip jelly on the table and almost laughed as she went back to her bedroom to dress.

Bess's bedroom and bathroom were just off the dining room. It was one of the things she and Joseph had liked most about the house. With two lively and inquisitive little girls, the privacy of a room away from their children's bedrooms had been a blessing. When Joseph was sick, he had been grateful for the peace and quiet of this room. That it looked out onto the garden was an added bonus, and he had spent hours looking at the flowers and watching the birds. Bess had made sure to keep the garden colorful for him, adding a forsythia bush and planting winter jasmine for a splash of bright yellow in the colder months. It was too cold in winter to open the windows, so it didn't matter that the jasmine had no scent. The man at Dobbie's also suggested laburnum, but she wasn't about to plant something poisonous, no matter how pretty.

Joseph loved the lilacs best, and by the time they bloomed, it was warm. On most days, Bess would open the back windows, and a pungent lilac fragrance would fill the bedroom. Then they would breathe deeply and try to forget the odors of the medicines and dressings that always seemed present. Bess knew he would have loved the hollyhocks, too. She had planted them early one spring, not realizing that it would be a year before they bloomed and that Joseph would not live to see them. They were lovely now, with stalks more than six feet tall and big white and maroon flowers, but she could not look at them without regret.

After Joseph died, Bess considered using the third bedroom upstairs. At first, she blamed her grief for the lethargy that prevented her from moving any of her belongings, but, in the end, the room she had shared with Joseph held too many happy memories to be abandoned. So the third upstairs bedroom, the largest bedroom in the house, remained unused. They called it the guest room, even though they never had guests.

Bess's morning chats with Joseph began when his illness kept him in bed most days. Before that, from the time they were first married, she had talked to him at night. He would hurry out of his clothes and into bed to wait for her. She would take her time, undressing slowly, hanging up her clothes, and talking to him. She knew she had his attention and was grateful that he never hurried her. By the time she crawled into bed next to him, he had made a warm nest in the sheets.

After he became ill, she would bring Joseph's breakfast to him in bed, and, as he ate, she would dress and talk to him. It was her favorite part of the day. Now she still talked to him as she dressed, and sometimes she even thought she had his attention.

"Joseph," she began, "I met a boy yesterday. Imagine. I stumbled on him before anybody else met him. Don't you think that must have been *beshert*?" Bess didn't say that when she first saw Douglas, just for an instant, she had felt thirty years younger, his shy, eager manner reminding her of Joseph, himself. "He couldn't even open a bank account, poor thing, so far from home, and without his mother or anybody else to look out for him.

"Then I thought he might be a boy who would appreciate Rose, and, even though he's a little younger than she is, I thought she might like him, too. So I asked him to dinner. I know it was impulsive, more of a hunch than anything else. But you always trusted my hunches." Bess slipped on her blue dress and buckled the belt. "Oh dear, it's on the last hole. Soon it won't fit around me at all. You always said the more of me to hug, the better, but I never believed you." Bess found her shoes on the floor of the closet and sat on the edge of the bed to tie them.

"He came to dinner last night, and I was right. He's a sweet boy from a good family. Not rich but with good values. I'm sure you would like him too, Joseph. And if Rose has a chance to know him without the pressure of dances and parties, she won't be so shy, and he'll see how kind and clever she is. Then maybe he'll marry her and take her home to the States with him, and she'll be safe.

"I've thought and thought about how to get them together, and I think the best way is to have him live here. You always told me not to push Rose, but this would just be a little arranging. Everything would be natural and relaxed if he was our boarder." Bess got up and smoothed her skirt. "Do you think the neighbors will gossip when they see a household of women take a male boarder? The thought of Mrs. Heath peering over her back fence and comparing notes about our comings and goings with the other busybodies is unbearable. I can't have the good name of our little family questioned. I haven't much else."

Bess looked out the window into the garden for a moment. "I know you help from where you are, but sometimes it's hard to know what to do right here. The news from Germany is terrible, and fate put this boy in my path. I've got to try everything."

Bess took her jewelry box from the top of her dresser and ran her hand across the highly polished lid, appreciating the perfectly smooth surface. "Some days, Joseph, I miss you more than I can say." Opening it carefully so the back hinge wouldn't break again, Bess chose her garnet brooch and pinned the wreath of little red stones on her dress.

"Addy will be a problem, of course. She's already trying to get herself noticed. I wish I had your way with her. I'll have to practice staying calm while keeping one step ahead. Once Rose is settled, I'll find a way to get Addy safe, too. Meanwhile, I'm sure she and I can keep the shop going without Rose." Bess sat in front the mirror at her dressing table. "He'll have to have this room, Joseph. I'll miss sleeping here, but the move upstairs will have a good reason."

Bess brushed her hair and twisted it into a bun. "And you'll come upstairs with me, of course," she said.

ROSE WAS UP AND DRESSED WHEN SHE HEARD THE KETTLE whistle. On her way through the dining room, she was aware of her mother mumbling to herself in her bedroom. When that strange behavior had begun the week after her father died, Rose had been worried. Once, feeling guilt and concern in equal measure, she had crept close to her mother's door and listened. The long lament of grief and loss she overheard made her embarrassed to be eavesdropping, almost as if she was spying on her parents when her father was alive, something she never would have done. Since Bess never mumbled to herself at other times of the day or in other places, the worry had passed. Now Rose barely noticed as she continued to the kitchen and brewed tea for the family.

When she noticed the rose hip jelly on the table, Rose wondered if Addy or her mother had put it out and decided that it must have been her mother. She opened the other jars of jam and put a spoon in each but she decided not to be the one to open the rose hip jelly. She didn't like rose hip jelly, anyway. The rich fruity flavor of raspberry preserves and the tang of orange marmalade were preferable.

By the time Addy got to the kitchen, Rose had had her first cup of tea and was measuring the oats and water into a saucepan for porridge.

"I'll do that, Rose," Addy said as she tied an apron over her skirt. "Don't get your work clothes dirty." Rose handed her the wooden spoon, and Addy stirred the porridge with one hand while she put water and three eggs into another pot and turned up the heat under them. When the water boiled, Addy turned the timer to let the sand fall through while she started the toast.

Just as the porridge was ready, Bess came out of her room dressed for the shop with her hair neatly braided and coiled in a bun at the back of her head. She took her place at the kitchen table, and Addy served her a bowl of porridge and a soft-boiled egg in an egg cup. Then she served Rose and herself, put the toast caddy on the table, and sat down.

"I hope you slept well," Bess said. Addy and Rose nodded. "There's something I need to tell you both." Addy glanced at Rose who also seemed mystified. Bess opened the rose hip jelly and spread some on her toast. "I've decided that if Douglas comes into the shop and he still hasn't found a room, I'm going to suggest that he boards with us."

"Did I hear you right?" Addy exclaimed. "You're going to ask a boy we hardly know to live here?"

"I'm sure you're surprised, Addy, but you needn't raise your voice. We've talked before about having a boarder, so this isn't a brand-new idea."

Neither of the girls reminded Bess that the assumption had always been that the boarder would be a woman with a quiet disposition and a meek manner.

"I'll move into the guest room, because, of course, I wouldn't put him upstairs with you, and he'll have the room down here. That way he'll have his privacy and so will we. I think he is a very nice boy, and we are in a position to help him if he needs it. We'll let fate decide. If we see him again and he hasn't found a place, I'll make the offer."

"But that's your room and Papa's room."

"A room is a room. Don't get sentimental, Addy. I'll be just as comfortable upstairs as I am down here." Bess poured herself a cup of tea and added milk from the pitcher on the table.

"Aren't you afraid there'll be talk if we take in a male boarder?" Rose asked.

Bess was so quick to answer that Addy knew she had considered this objection.

"Of course not. They know what kind of people we are, and they know we have a downstairs bedroom and that I'll be upstairs with the two of you. And if some people talk, well, let those nosy parkers say what they want. I don't see how there's more danger than in any other situation. We all know what happened to the Ferrington girl. That family would have been better off if they had had that boy under their own roof where they could have kept an eye on him. We've never given the neighborhood reason to talk about us before, and we'll give them no reason now. And Douglas doesn't seem like the kind of boy who will give them reason, either."

Rose remained pensive. She must be thinking about the shop, Addy thought. Rose wouldn't care about gossip in the neighborhood, but if it reached the ears of her customers, Rose would worry.

For several minutes, the three of them ate in silence. Bess sprinkled brown sugar on her porridge and ate it neatly in small mouthfuls while Addy ignored her cereal and spread a large scoop of rose hip jelly on a piece of toast.

Rose helped herself to another cup of tea and said, "I imagine we'll be busy today. Even so, I'd like to find time to put a display of the new blouses in the window. I think they're going to be just the thing this fall, and I want customers to see that we have them."

Talk of the shop seemed to shake everybody awake.

"I'll come by a bit earlier this afternoon," Addy said, "and help Mama with the customers while you do the window."

"That would be a big help, Addy. Thanks."

"And I'll try on one of the new blouses, since I'll surely be needing something new myself this fall." Addy heard her mother sigh, and she thought that Rose chuckled, though she hadn't said anything funny.

After Bess and Rose left for the shop, Addy made herself another cup of tea, and while it was brewing, she opened the rose hip jelly and brought it to her nose. She inhaled once and then again before putting the jar back on the table. Disappointing, she thought. It smells dense and pungent in an odd way, but not floral. Definitely not floral.

Addy took her tea outside and sat on the back stoop. Birds bustled about the hedge and flitted in and out of the foliage, and three large squirrels chased each other up and down the apple tree. Most gardeners thought that squirrels were pests, but Addy took some satisfaction in the fact that her squirrels looked sleek and well fed.

This had been Bess's garden, and the garden seat under the apple tree emphasized her claim. Years ago, when Addy was just a little girl, several large, mysterious packages had arrived for her father. They sat for a week in the dining room, and nobody was allowed to touch them. At last, on Sunday, Joseph had taken them to the backyard and sternly told the family not to come into the garden or watch from the windows. Bess had laughed and promised to keep her eyes on her knitting; Rose had busied herself in the front room where she wouldn't be tempted to look; but Addy sneaked up to Rose's bedroom and peeked through the curtains. She watched as her father unpacked several large pieces of wood, all carefully marked, and an envelope with instructions and a picture. Her father worked all day, and just before dinner he invited them into the garden. A heavy, rustic chair with long curved armrests sat under the apple tree, and he ceremoniously announced that this was their mother's "garden throne" and that she alone was allowed to sit in it. He had also built a sturdy bench for the rest of the family. As everybody sat in their designated places, Joseph said, "You're a regal woman, Bess," and she had answered, "If I'm a queen, you must be my prince." Addy remembered this occasion well because it was the only time she could remember seeing her mother kiss her father.

Addy and Rose had not been allowed to play in the garden until they learned to be gentle with the plants and careful where they stepped. So it had always been a quiet garden with no running around or loud voices where, eventually, Rose helped Addy serve tea to her dolls.

Addy particularly liked the garden in the spring. She loved to see the shy little snowdrops appear, and the crocuses, which were just as small, open boldly to the sun. She approved of the way the anemone stole the last of winter's chill for its blue color and admired the peony for adding a touch of glamour with its elegant red blossoms.

It had been Bess's idea to plant the brilliant blue flowers that spread along the base of the wall and reminded her of Russia, but now it was Addy who read *Amateur Gardening* and cared for the garden. There were many changes she would have liked to make, but Bess always had the final word. This year Addy had been allowed to plant muscari at the base of the apple tree. Its flowers looked like clusters of grapes on stalks that marched around the sturdy trunk.

Addy decided to gather lilacs to bring into the house. She put her teacup in the kitchen sink and took the big shears and a flat round basket from the back closet. As she pulled her garden clogs over her shoes, she wondered if she would be traipsing about the house in muddy clogs with her hair pushed back behind her ears and carrying the big shears if Douglas was living with them. Thinking about her appearance would be just one complication of having Douglas in the house. It also worried Addy that he would have plenty of time to get to know Rose and become impressed with her intelligence and charmed by her humor. Then her plain looks and lack of flair might become unimportant. Of course, he might seem like a little brother to Rose. That was a comforting thought until Addy realized that he might become like an older brother to her. She already reminded him of his little sister.

Addy stood for a time looking at the lilac bush and enjoying the scent. No other plant in the garden combined such beautiful flowers, abundant blooms, and powerful fragrance. It had been her father's favorite flower, and her mother had placed a vase of fresh lilacs in his room every day during the last weeks of his illness. For a long time after her father died, lilacs were not permitted in the house. It was the flower Addy loved best, too, so she was pleased when her mother relented and allowed her to bring them in again.

Addy began to cut small branches and rest them carefully in the basket. Did Douglas like lilacs? There was no way to know if he noticed flowers at all, given his gift of jelly the night before.

That gift had been for her mother, and, now that Addy thought of it, he had focused on Bess all evening. He only looked at me or Rose when Mama directed his attention to us, and then his interest seemed in response to gratifying her request. Why did he do that? Surely, he didn't plan on marrying her! Addy laughed out loud at the picture of her plump, little mother done up in a frilly bridal gown standing next to a solemn Douglas with his silly moustache. Maybe she and Rose would wear short dresses and carry baskets of rose petals to strew in the path of the happy couple. Or maybe they would carry jars of rose hip jelly to distribute to the guests. Wouldn't the neighbors talk then!

Bess had seemed as focused on Douglas as he had been focused on her. That made more sense. But she hadn't asked about his father or his brothers or his friends or if he was a good student; she only wanted to know about his mother. She only wanted to find out if he was a good son. A good son?

Addy had heard mention of a son only once before when she stood with her mother and Rose at her father's burial. In her grief, Bess had cried out to her husband as if they were alone.

"I'm sorry we never had the son you wanted," she had sobbed. "I'm sorry, Joseph. Forgive me. Whatever was my fault, forgive me."

Embarrassed and frightened by her mother's outburst, Addy had held tight to Rose's hand and watched her mother sway and weep with such abandon that Mrs. Thomas, their next-door neighbor, had grabbed her coat from behind, afraid that she might fall into the grave, herself. That seemed to waken Bess to her surroundings, and she quickly composed herself.

There were no more outbursts then or during the week following the funeral when the three of them stayed in the house, and people came to visit and bring food. That had been a long, lonely, sad week. Women from the neighborhood and from the synagogue did stop by, and they were nice to Addy and Rose, but they were few in number. Every evening families from the synagogue visited, and the men led a prayer service before they left. They would express their condolences to Bess saying, "A lovely man," or "Nobody ever said a bad word about Joseph." When they added, "You girls were lucky to have a dad as fine your dad," Rose and Addy would nod. Mostly Bess was quiet, but one evening Mr. Fein said, "I imagine you'll be looking to sell the shop, Mrs. Kaminsky."

"You'll be imagining wrong, Mr. Fein," Bess had answered sharply. "Rose and I will manage the shop without a problem. I promised Joseph that we would not abandon his lovely shop, and we won't. I'll keep both his shop and his daughters safe."

"I'm glad to hear that," Mr. Fein quickly said. "You're a grand mother and a strong woman with a fine head for business. I'm sure the shop will continue to be a great success."

The neighbors stopped coming by as soon as the week of mourning was over. Bess said it was a relief not to have people underfoot all the time, that their little family was all they needed.

As if to prove her point, Bess and Rose reopened the shop a week after the funeral. Rose had already worked with her father for three years before his illness and, after his death, she took over the management of the shop with ease. Addy knew she was expected to do the housework after school, and her cooking lessons had started then. At first, she turned on the oven and put the casserole in to bake when she got home from school. Eventually, she cut vegetables or made a salad or fixed the soup. By the time she was fourteen, Addy was proud that she was the only girl she knew who could put a complete dinner on the table and have it taste good, too. Bess had proved that their little family was, indeed, all they needed.

If it's all we need, Addy thought, why do we need Douglas? Because Mama always trusts her hunches. One of her hunches convinced Papa to settle in Edinburgh, and another hunch persuaded him to buy the house on Glenorchy Terrace. It was a hunch that encouraged them to risk their savings and open the shop. So it was probably a hunch that gave her confidence in Douglas. That and the fact that fate had put him in her path. Douglas was to be either a son or a son-in-law. Addy was sure of that. She hoped that Bess didn't get too focused on turning him into a son. Douglas already had a mother he said he adored. One mother was enough for anybody, and Addy knew her mother could feel like one mother too many all by herself.

If Douglas lived in the house, he needed to know that she wasn't looking for a big brother. She was looking for a beau, and he was useful either as that man, himself, or as an opportunity to meet other medical students.

THREE DAYS LATER, DOUGLAS HAD YET TO STOP BY THE shop. At home, none of the three women mentioned his name. Rose seemed focused on business issues and the book she had just finished reading, *Miss Mole*. Every morning at breakfast she entertained Bess and Addy with Miss Mole's latest adventures, reporting with approval Miss Mole's delight in her independent life and her liaison with a man unworthy of her love. Bess expressed shock, but Rose thought that such a woman should not be judged by conventional standards. It always amazed Addy that, in the context of talking about books, Rose felt free to disagree with their mother with impunity.

After praising Miss Mole's proud independence throughout the book, Rose was disappointed that, in the end, Miss Mole is saved from loneliness and despair by the devotion of a good man. Bess, on the other hand, was relieved and said she would like to borrow the book and read it for herself now that she knew it turned out well.

Addy enjoyed hearing the daily installments of whatever Rose was reading, although it annoyed her that nobody listened to her opinions except in the distracted way they might listen to a child permitted to add a comment to adult conversation. But since Douglas had come to dinner, Addy didn't care if they ignored her. She spent her time wondering and worrying about the possibilities and perils of having Douglas in the house. Would he notice and be grateful that she fixed his breakfast? Perhaps he would smile and say, "Breakfast has become my favorite meal of the day, Addy. I never knew it could be so delicious," and the two of them would have a quiet conversation about the joys of breakfast. Or would he talk about Rose's books, ignoring her comments like her mother and Rose did? No. He would listen and say, "What an interesting idea, Addy. I never would have thought of that."

Addy wished that Bess or Rose would bring up his name, but neither did. Even when she pointed out that they would soon need more rose hip jelly, neither of them reacted. Addy thought that Rose was probably not think-ing about Douglas, but she knew her mother better than to assume Bess had put him out of her mind. Nonetheless, Bess bustled about as usual, ruling her tiny fiefdom with her tiny iron hand.

ON TUESDAY MORNING OF THE FOLLOWING WEEK, BESS appeared in the kitchen as Addy sat at the kitchen table leafing through the latest issue of *Amateur Gardening* and planning to reshape the garden in her image.

"Addy, every time I come home in the morning, you're at the table sipping tea or reading magazines. What's that you've got there now?"

Addy held up the magazine so that her mother could see the cover, and Bess's expression softened. "I'd like to try gladiolus for color in the early summer. They're tender flowers, and I want to do it right." Addy leafed through the magazine until she found a picture of yellow and scarlet gladiolus to show her mother.

"That's fine, Addy, but there are more important things to think about right now."

Addy closed the magazine and pushed it to the corner of the table. She knew that whatever was on her mother's mind was more important than anything on her own mind, and that whatever important thing was on Bess's mind was so important that she had hurried home from the shop. Addy suspected what that might be. Douglas.

"Douglas came into the shop this morning." Bess waited for Addy to react and seemed annoyed when Addy maintained her neutral expression. "Don't think I believe that look for one minute, young lady. You have to get up early in the morning to put one over on me. I know exactly what you are thinking."

Addy smiled as if to acknowledge Bess's acumen and asked, "What did he want? Does he still need a place to stay?"

"Yes, he does. And I offered him our downstairs bedroom. He refused at first and said that he couldn't put us to so much trouble, but I said that we were planning to have a boarder in any case, and we all thought he was the best choice. He still seemed reluctant, but I managed to convince him that he was doing us a favor and that we would all be more relaxed and feel safer with a man in the house, and then he seemed pleased to say yes."

"What did Rose say?"

"Rose? She didn't say anything. She was in the back unpacking a box of ribbon."

Addy could just imagine the scene. Her mother smiling and persuading, just as she did with customers, and Douglas convincing her that her powers of persuasion were winning him over. Addy knew that her mother liked nothing better than to be agreed with, especially to be agreed with after changing your mind. Though she had never seen Rose persuade customers, Addy had tried her mother's technique and found that it worked for her, too. Customers seemed to like being led along until they found themselves spending a little more than they had intended for just the thing to make their snooty neighbors take notice. Either Douglas knew her mother well, or he had known women like her before, or he was naive and lucky. In any case, now that he would be living in the house, Addy planned to find out. There was a lot to be learned from watching Douglas, and she intended to make the most of the opportunity. Even better, since she knew he was susceptible to persuading, maybe there would be a chance to do some persuading, herself.

"Addy. Whatever are you daydreaming about? You need to get busy. I'm going to stay home today to move my things upstairs, and you're going to help me. Tomorrow you can get his room ready. He'll be here on Saturday in the morning. He asked me if that would disturb us, but I told him we aren't so religious that having him move in on Saturday is a problem."

Addy wondered if Douglas knew they kept the shop open on Saturdays; she felt sure he would approve. Would he also approve of Friday night dinners? Her father had always insisted on a traditional Friday night dinner including Torah stories and

N.R. King

songs. When Rose and Addy were little, he would go to the dining room windows and pretend to scold neighbors who had gathered on the lawn to hear them sing Sabbath songs. "Shoo, now," he would say, rapping on the glass. "Away with you. I won't have you standing on the lawn, peering in the windows, and listening to the beautiful voices of my daughters."

Then Rose and Addy would look at each other and giggle, Addy with delight at thinking their songs were that lovely, and Rose with pleasure at their father's sweet, good humor. Would Douglas do that for his children or would he be a father who overlooked the Sabbath completely? And what if he neglected more than the Sabbath? Is it possible that he eats ham? What if he plans to eat ham in his house when he has a family? Addy didn't like that idea, and quickly decided that failing to keep the Sabbath was one thing, but eating ham was another thing, altogether. Douglas would certainly not expect to be served ham in his own house.

"And another thing," Bess continued, "don't tell him that the room was mine. I let him think it was the room we were saving for the boarder."

Addy had lots to think about but no time to think right then. She was busy the rest of the day going up and down the stairs with handfuls of clothes and belongings and settling her mother into the guest room. The next day, as she worked getting Douglas's room ready, Addy wondered what it would be like to have that deep, rumbling voice living in the house. Would she get used to it the way she had once been used to hearing her father's voice, or would she be shocked every time Douglas opened his mouth? Addy wished her father was still alive so she could hear them talk together and could judge whether or not Douglas's voice was pleasant compared to her father's. But, of course, if her father was still alive, Douglas would not be moving in.

Addy spread the bottom sheet on the bed with a flick of her wrists and smoothed it down. A regular little chambermaid, she thought, and worried that Douglas would see her as a servant girl. Would that be better than being compared to his little sister? Addy couldn't decide. Maybe he won't notice me at all, and that would be even worse. Of course, he's not being asked to live here to take notice of me. He's being lured here to take notice of Rose. Addy was quite certain she had guessed her mother's plot and then reminded herself that her mother was full of secrets and feints and, if all else failed, outright lies. Still, it did seem obvious that Rose was the point, and Addy worried that Douglas would like Rose and then worried that he wouldn't, and then hoped that he wouldn't. I'm much prettier, and I can cook more things than Rose, she reasoned. I'll be a much better wife. But what if Douglas would rather have somebody who works hard and reads a lot? Addy couldn't believe that was true. No man would rather have a bookworm than a good cook. So far, though, he didn't seem to have noticed either of them. Maybe he just wants a room, so a household where one sister is too old and one sister is too young is perfect. The cad. He could flatter Mama, joke with Rose, and tease me while he sleeps well and eats well for five years before sailing home alone. He'll not get away with that, Addy thought. Not if I have any say in the matter.

With the bed made, the towels laid out, the curtains freshly hung, and the dusting done, Addy had no more excuses to linger in what was already known as Douglas's room. What would her father think if he knew another man was going to sleep in his bed and look through his windows into the garden? Addy smoothed the bedspread one more time and pulled the curtains closed before she left the room.

>——>>|————|<<——<

Friday night dinner was one of the few religious traditions that persisted in Bess's home after Joseph's death. On the Friday night before Douglas was to move in, Sabbath candles burned on the dining room table, and the family ate a traditional meal of roast chicken and potato kugel. At the end of the meal, Bess made what Addy thought of later as her "proper young ladies speech."

"I'm sure I don't need to remind either of you that you are expected to behave in a proper manner at all times when Douglas is here. No more coming down for breakfast on Sunday in nighties or walking through the house barefoot or with your hair down. Douglas will need his privacy, and he'll need peace and quiet to study. There will be no bothering him. Especially you, Addy."

Rose looked amused by this proclamation, but Addy was incensed. She felt like a little girl reprimanded before she had done anything wrong. "Of course, I'm not going to bother him," she said. "And he had better not bother me."

"That's enough of that attitude. You'll be nice and that's that. Now clear the dishes."

Addy lay awake that night formulating her plans for the morning. Since Rose and Mama will be at the shop, I'll be the one to greet Douglas and welcome him to the house. After he's settled, we'll have a lovely chat over lunch. I'll need to make sure he knows that I prepared his room and recognizes the hard work and expertise it took to make it so pretty and comfortable. But that I didn't mind at all.

Addy woke early the next morning and dressed with care. She chose her sensible green skirt and the matching sweater she had made herself. Maybe there would be an opportunity to work her success with the difficult pattern into conversation while she helped Douglas unpack and get settled. Her first clue that her plan to greet Douglas was doomed came when her mother did not go to the shop with Rose. The final blow fell when Douglas came to the door with his trunk and a box of books, and Bess immediately sent her to the shop to help Rose. Addy barely had time to give him a charming smile before he was inside, and she was on the sidewalk.

Addy spent the day wondering if he appreciated how nicely the room had been prepared for him, and if her mother had taken credit for the freshly laundered bedspread and the crisp, clean curtains. Of course, it could be that nobody got credit because men don't notice such things. Maybe when she got home, she would ask him if he was comfortable and if he liked the view of the garden and maybe he would like a tour of the garden, and she could tell him about her plans to plant gladiolus. Unfortunately, by the time she and Rose got home in the afternoon, Douglas had moved in and gone out again.

As the family settled into a routine that included a boarder, it seemed to Addy that Douglas must have been subject to a "proper young gentleman" speech to match the speech that she and Rose had heard. Douglas was always calm, polite, and respectful. He never left his room unless he was fully dressed, carefully shaved except for his silly mustache, and with his hair neatly combed until the curls began to spring free as they dried. He didn't come into the kitchen for breakfast until Bess was downstairs, and though he treated all of them with kindness, he showed Bess a special regard. Whenever Addy came upon the two of them sitting in the living room or at the dining room table talking together, her mother was smiling or laughing, listening to his tales of medical school, and giving advice.

Douglas joined in the breakfast book discussions even

if he hadn't read the book. He complained that they always talked about the book Rose was reading, and teased that he was going to make them discuss the book he was reading. Then they would find themselves fascinated by the functions of the kidney or arguing about diseases of the skin. He also told them about medical school and made everybody laugh when he said that his lab group in anatomy had named their cadaver Ernest so they could say they were working in dead earnest.

Addy's efforts to study Douglas were frustrated by the fact that Douglas wasn't home enough to be studied. To her disappointment, he always left the house before Bess left for the shop and was gone all day and well into the evening. He explained that he had to study and see patients. Often, Bess set aside his dinner, and Addy assumed he ate it alone before going to bed. His dishes were always washed and put away when she came into the kitchen in the morning.

Occasionally on the weekends, Addy heard Douglas open the back door very quietly and tiptoe to his room late at night, but the family never heard anything of his weekend adventures, if there were adventures. On Sundays, if he didn't have to be at the hospital, he read and studied in his room or helped with the heavy cleaning in the house. Sometimes Bess sent him and Rose on an errand or to the market, and then he helped carry packages.

In spite of his busy schedule at school, Douglas also cleaned the shop after closing. Addy asked her mother why Douglas was doing so much in the shop and at home and was told that he is a helpful person who sees himself as a member of the family. She asked Douglas the same question and got the same answer. It sounded rehearsed.

Every so often, Douglas and Rose went sightseeing because

Bess said it was important for him to feel at home in Edinburgh. They visited the castle, walked along High Street, sat in the Princes Street Gardens, and climbed to the top of the Scott Monument. Although her mother must have approved of these outings, Addy noticed that Bess had a clear idea of how long each excursion should take and grew anxious as the time she expected them home approached. They were only late once, and then only a little late, so Bess seemed less concerned as the months went by.

Try as she might, Addy never got to go along with Rose and Douglas because Bess always had something for her to do at home. The day they visited the castle, her mother insisted that Addy clean her closet.

"That can wait for another time," Addy protested. "I want to see the castle with Douglas and Rose."

"You've seen the castle before, but I've never seen the likes of your closet before, so don't argue with me and get busy." That was the day they came home late, and Rose blamed Douglas for having no stamina at all.

"He's as slow as slow can be," she laughed.

Douglas was laughing, too, as he came to his own defense. "On the way there, Rose walked me down the stairs at the end of Vennel Street, across Grassmarket, and then up Granny's Green Steps. By the time we got to the castle, I could hardly catch my breath."

"You'll not survive in Edinburgh if you can't climb hills and go up a few stairs," Rose said.

Bess set out the soup and sandwiches she had made for supper, and they all sat down together at the kitchen table to eat. "So how did you like our castle?" she asked.

"I thought it would be a big building, but it's really a small town. When the warden found out I was an American, he made sure to show us where the prisoners captured in the

American Revolution were kept. I wondered if he planned to assign me a hammock and leave me down there."

"Didn't you like the king's ear best?" Addy asked, naming her favorite part of the castle, a square opening high on the dining room wall where the king would leave a servant to eavesdrop on his guests after he went to bed. Addy often wished she had an Addy's ear in every room throughout the house so she could hear what went on in her absence.

Douglas laughed. "I can see why you might like that best, Addy, but I liked the new War Memorial best. It's a beautiful building, and with the names of those killed in The Great War engraved on the pedestal of the stone casket, it's sad and magnificent at the same time."

Addy took no more part in the conversation. What did he mean when he said he knew I'd like the king's ear best? That I'm a child who likes to snoop? When have I ever snooped on him? And everybody likes the king's ear best, if they'd only admit it.

"I thought you were going to say the Crown Room," Rose said. "It was all I could do to get you out of there." Rose turned to her mother. "I think he had designs on the jewels. And if The Stone of Destiny had been there, I expect he would have had a seat so we could crown him King of England."

"That does have a nice ring to it," Douglas said. "From now on, you may all refer to me as King Douglas."

Everybody laughed and helped clear the supper dishes. While Addy and Rose cleaned the kitchen, Douglas tuned in the radio in the living room, and Bess picked up her knitting.

Addy was just coming into the parlor with a magazine when she heard her mother say, "I'm glad you had a good time with Rose this afternoon."

"Rose is a nice girl. She's easy to have a good time with,"

Douglas answered.

Just a nice girl who is easy to be with? Addy didn't hear the usual unconstrained response Douglas made when Bess asked about his schoolwork, and she didn't hear an attachment to Rose. Maybe he doesn't want Mama to know that he's only sightseeing with Rose because it seems to be expected. How thoughtful.

Since she wasn't allowed to go on excursions with Douglas, Addy had only the time he was in the house to create her special relationship with him. At first, she worked to get his attention by wearing all her skirts and blouses, one after another for several weeks without repeating any combination exactly, though the variation was often as subtle as a different brooch or a new barrette. Douglas didn't seem to notice, but her mother remarked that she was making unusually creative use of her wardrobe.

Early one morning, Addy was surprised to find herself alone in the kitchen with Douglas. Neither Rose nor Bess had appeared yet, and Addy was presented with her first opportunity for a private conversation with him. Previously, her mother, who seemed to have a sixth sense whenever Addy tried to put herself in his path, had always interrupted them and made it a threesome before it had even become a twosome. But now Addy had no obstacles, though she knew they could be interrupted any minute. Especially if they stayed in the kitchen.

"It seems we're the early birds this morning, Douglas. How would you like a peek at my garden before breakfast?"

"Sure, Addy. Let's tour the garden."

Addy opened the back door carefully and let Douglas precede her down the steps before she closed the door as quietly as possible. The silence in the kitchen might convince her mother that nobody was up yet, and the longer her mother failed to realize that she and Douglas were out of the house, the better.

The garden did its part by presenting its lovely colors gleaming in the morning dew. Now Addy needed to do her part and get Douglas to notice.

"Do you have a garden at home?" she asked.

"We don't have anything like this. Our backyard is much smaller, and there's nothing planted there. Some grass comes up by itself, but that's about it."

"There's a shame. It's lovely to have flowers about, don't you think?"

"Flowers are pretty and they smell nice, but I have to say, I don't know much about them."

"Come, then, let me show you around."

Addy walked Douglas through the garden, naming the flowers and describing how she cared for them.

"You know a lot about plants, Addy."

For the first time, Addy thought he sounded just a little bit impressed with her. See, she felt like saying, I'm not only pretty, I'm smart, too.

"Let's sit on the bench for a few minutes before we go in," Addy suggested.

Douglas agreed, and the two of them sat down.

"I'm going to plant gladiolus soon. They are very hard to grow, and I need to do it just right. But they'll add so many bright colors to the garden that the hard work will be worth it."

Douglas looked around. "I bet Rose likes to come out here to read."

"All of us like the garden, Douglas," Bess said, bursting out the back door and bustling over to join them. "This was my project, but now Addy tends it because Rose and I are too busy in the shop to have time for a garden."

Addy sighed. If only she'd had a little longer.

Addy had no more opportunities for private conversations with Douglas. So, whenever possible, she was careful to smile at him in a beguiling fashion and laugh if she thought he was trying to be funny. But he was as oblivious to her special smiles as he was to her outfits. Once, he did notice that she had braided her hair and coiled it on top of her head. It had pleased her when he said, "Ah, Addy, that's a pretty hairdo." But her pleasure was cut short when he added, "If you meet my little sister, you'll have to teach her how to comb her hair that way."

"Don't you think she's a bit young for this style?" Addy had responded.

Douglas looked surprised and scrutinized her hairdo more carefully. "Now that you mention it, I think you're right. This would be too adult for her," he said.

Addy was pleased. When you take a careful look, I'm not such a child, she thought. You should take a careful look more often.

ONE MORNING AT BREAKFAST, DOUGLAS MENTIONED THAT he planned to go to a party of Jewish medical students. Addy knew that Scottish girls also went to such parties, and without thinking, blurted out, "May I come along?"

"What an absurd thing to ask!" her mother exclaimed. "You may not. You are much too young to be thinking of any such thing. I can't imagine where you got the idea that you could go to parties at fifteen." Addy raised her head and opened her mouth as if to respond, and Bess quickly added, "I don't want to hear how you'll be sixteen in a few months."

Addy looked down at her hands in her lap. She knew that

Bess wouldn't stop until she ran out of steam.

"You were a bit younger than the other girls when you finished school, so you'll have a bit longer to wait than they have before you'll be going to parties. That could be some time away if you don't become a more sensible girl than you are this morning."

Addy blushed with fury at her mother for humiliating her in front of Douglas, and with anger at herself for letting it happen. When will I learn to hold my tongue, she thought. It's not Douglas's permission I need, it's hers. If I'm stupid enough to ask to go, I should be smart enough to ask in private. I still wouldn't be going to the party, but at least I'd have escaped a public scolding.

"Rose can go if she wants," Bess added.

Douglas seemed to have no taste for prolonging the discussion of the party, but he quickly said, "Join me if you want, Rose."

"That's very kind, Douglas, but I have plans for Saturday night, and I don't usually enjoy parties."

"If your plans change, Rose, perhaps you'll be able to join Douglas," Bess said.

"That's true, but unlikely, Mother," Rose said.

"If you do change your mind, Rose," Douglas said, "just let me know. You're more than welcome to come with me. And in a year or two, you'll be able to come along, too, Addy."

Addy smiled at him, but Bess looked none too pleased.

Near the end of his first year, Douglas became more and more quiet and spent more and more time in his room or at school. Bess excused him from his tasks in the house and at the shop saying he had to study and they would have to do without his help for a few weeks. When his final test results put him near the top of the class, Addy was surprised at how proud she felt. In fact, everybody was proud. Bess announced that dinner on Friday night would be a celebration of his accomplishments. Addy made the same dinner they had had on his first night with them so many months before and was pleased when Douglas noticed.

"This is as delicious as I remember, Addy," he said. "Maybe you should get a job as a cook instead of a shop girl."

"She's got a job as a cook right here," Bess said. "And we need her in the shop."

"You and Rose manage without me most of the time," Addy said. "I was thinking maybe I would work at Leith Provident or maybe even Jenners. I could learn a lot in a big store, and I would have a salary to bring home."

"It sounds like you're getting a little full of yourself. You're needed in the shop, and that's where you will work. I don't want to hear another word about it."

At that moment, Rose got up from the table, went to her room, and returned with a long, thin box which she put down in front of Douglas. "This is for Douglas for doing such a fine job during his first year of medical school," she said.

Everybody looked surprised. Addy was most surprised by the look on her mother's face. It was clear that Bess had not known about this gift. Douglas didn't seem to know what to say, and Addy could see he was blushing. She hadn't known that men could blush.

When Douglas did try to talk, his stammer seemed a little worse. "You didn't need to get me anything. You do so much for me already."

"Well, open it," Bess said, "so we can all see what it is."

Douglas opened the box and found a red and black tartan scarf inside.

"I know you fancy yourself a Scot now that you've been

here a year," Rose said. "So I've made you a regular member of the Stewart clan. You can't do better than that." She smiled as he wrapped the scarf around his neck with a flourish. "It becomes you," she said.

"Thank you, Rose," Douglas said. "It's the perfect gift to keep me warm and make me feel at home. I'll treasure it."

Now it was Rose's turn to blush.

When Addy got up to clear the table, Bess said, "Wait a minute, Addy. Bring me four little glasses from the breakfront and my bottle of Lochan Ora." Bess poured a bit into each glass and said, "I propose a toast." Everybody stood and raised their glasses. "Mazel Tov to Douglas on his accomplishments." Bess paused. She seemed to have something else to say, but then simply added, "*L'Chaim!*" and sat down. Everybody sipped their drinks, and the table was quiet. Addy loved the taste of the Scotch, warm and smooth with just a little tingle. And she noticed that her mother had poured her almost as much as the others.

Douglas went out after dinner, and Addy assumed that his classmates were having celebrations of their own now that the term was over. The three women sat in the front room together. Bess knitted, as usual. For once, she was making something for herself, a new sweater in a pale blue yarn. Rose was reading a book. They both seemed content, but Addy wished she was doing something more exciting than sitting at home. How Rose could spend nearly every evening with their mother after spending every day in the shop with her was beyond Addy's understanding.

"What's that you're reading, Rose?" Addy asked.

"I've just started *Babbitt* by Sinclair Lewis." Rose held up the book cover for her to see. "He won the Nobel Prize in Literature a couple of years ago, the first American to win it."

"Is it a good story so far?" Bess asked.

"If this is what life is like in America, I don't see how anybody survives," Rose said.

Bess knitted for a few minutes before saying, "You need to find other books to read. I'm sure that not everybody in America is like the characters in that book. Some of the people must be happy to live there."

Addy picked up her gardening magazine and leafed through it again.

"Are you looking for something to read, Addy?" Rose asked. "You might like some of my books. Take anything on my shelf that looks good to you."

"Thanks, Rose," Addy said. "Right now, I'm trying to choose plants for the summer. I'm thinking of planting a new tree."

"There'll be no new trees," her mother said. "That garden is getting too crowded as it is. Just work on keeping everything already there alive."

THE NEXT TIME ADDY DUSTED ROSE'S ROOM, SHE LOOKED over the books on Rose's shelf, but there were so many that she didn't know how to choose one. When she finished her dusting, she lingered, as usual, over the wooden box on the dresser. Her mother had one just like it. After her father made Bess's jewelry box, he made one for Rose and gave it to her on her twelfth birthday. He had worked on it for weeks, and the pale blond wood shone with layers of lacquer. The hinges and the ornate lock were gold, and there was a tiny gold key that Rose left in the lock. Her father had promised Addy a wooden box for her twelfth birthday, but he hadn't lived long enough to keep his word. Addy had always coveted Rose's box. Not so much because she wanted it instead of Rose, but because she wished she had one, too. Her father had left her mother two daughters, and he had left Rose the shop, but he hadn't left her anything. Not even a lacquer box.

Duty

1936

A T FIRST, HAVING A MEDICAL STUDENT LIVING IN THE house made Addy a bit of a celebrity among her friends. They asked for stories about his daily habits, and Addy regaled them with tales of breakfast conversations and moments alone in the garden with him.

"He's very clever and studious," Addy told them. "But he appreciates a pretty face and a good meal as much as the next fellow."

"Was it just the two of you in the garden?"

Addy nodded solemnly.

"What did you find to say to him?" Eileen asked.

"He wanted to know about the plants and flowers, and I told him how I care for the garden. He has nothing like it at home. We sat together on the bench chatting for a long time."

"Did he try to get fresh?"

"That's a nasty thing to say. Of course not. He's not that kind of boy, and he knows I'm not that kind of girl."

"Isn't it hard to always have a strange man about?" Eileen persisted. "How ever do you manage?"

"You get used to it," Addy responded airily. "It's not difficult to always look your best."

"Did he tell you you're pretty?"

"He's not so crude as that. But he did say that, one day, he'd like me to show his little sister how to dress and do her hair."

"How are you ever going to meet her?"

Addy shrugged. "Perhaps he has plans. Perhaps we both do."

Eventually, Eileen's persistent questioning reached the limit of Addy's ability to embroider her encounters with Douglas, and he was pronounced to behave just like a big brother and of no more interest than their own. Addy hadn't realized, having no experience with big brothers, that she had unwittingly painted such a picture for them.

WITH NO OPPORTUNITY TO CREATE A RELATIONSHIP WITH Douglas, Addy turned her attention to cooking wonderful dinners, helping in the shop, and learning to dance from her friend Harriet's older sister.

"It's true that he's a bit of a bore," she told Harriet. "He treats Rose and me just like little sisters, even though Rose is older."

When Harriet wondered aloud if Douglas was interested in Rose, Addy scoffed at the idea. Still, after Harriet's remark, Addy began to watch for signs that Douglas favored Rose. Could it be that a romance was flourishing under her very nose? They did go sightseeing and on errands together, and he was the one who suggested that he and Rose cook Sunday dinner for the family. Addy had been peeved at the time that he never offered to cook with her until she decided that her expertise had warned him off. When it came to the kitchen, Rose was enough of an amateur to match his equally limited experience.

Nobody else was allowed in the kitchen when they cooked because they said they wanted dinner to be a surprise. It never was a surprise, though, because Douglas could only cook steak, and Rose always made potatoes and a vegetable to go along with the meat. Mostly, it seemed to Addy, they laughed and dropped things. Cleaning up after the meal took as long as the preparations and the dinner combined, but since Rose and Douglas did that themselves, too, Addy couldn't complain about the mess they made in her kitchen.

Even though he spent more time with Rose, Addy didn't notice him being any kinder or more pleasant to her than he was to the rest of the family. If there is anybody he favors, Addy decided, it's Mama. He honors her as if she were the most important Jewish matriarch in Edinburgh.

It didn't escape Addy's notice, however, that the more time Rose spent with Douglas, the happier she seemed. She laughed even more than usual, and Addy thought she looked almost pretty, though Rose hadn't changed anything specific about her appearance. She was also more energetic and had offered to stay late at the shop so that Bess could come home earlier.

"Good," Bess had said, "gets me off my feet sooner." But she had made it clear that Rose was to come home as soon as she locked up at closing time.

One afternoon, Rose did not return home at the expected time, and Bess became worried.

"Call the shop," Addy said, "and see why she's delayed."

"The shop phone is only for business. You know the rule."

"But this is different. You should call her. That's what Douglas would do."

"A rule is a rule for a reason," her mother said, but didn't elaborate on what the reason might be.

After another ten minutes, Bess broke her own rule without comment and called the shop. There was no answer. She told Addy to keep dinner warm and was buttoning her coat when Rose came in.

Bess rushed to meet her at the door. "Where have you been? I've been worried half to death."

"I'm sorry you worried," Rose said, taking off her coat and hat and putting them in the hall closet. She took her mother's coat and hung it up, too. "The new gloves arrived, and I decided to arrange them in the showcase. The shop wasn't busy so I got a good start, and I decided to stay after closing to finish the job."

"It's not safe for you to be in the shop all by yourself," Bess said.

"Don't worry. I was perfectly safe."

"Not by yourself after closing."

"I wasn't by myself. Douglas came by to sweep up."

Addy was shocked. What was Rose thinking? Maybe it's the way we see him as a sort of brother that makes her think nothing of saying they were alone together. Even so, it seemed like reckless behavior to Addy.

"I forgot that Wednesday is his day to clean," Bess said. She paused before adding, "I know you're a sensible girl, Rose, but we need to be aware of what the neighbors might say."

Rose was late coming home the next two Wednesdays in a row, and Bess told her that Addy would be helping in the store on Wednesday afternoons from now on so she wouldn't be delayed getting home.

The following Wednesday afternoon, Addy worked in the shop. She expected to see Douglas, but he didn't come to clean.

"I thought Douglas cleaned on Wednesdays," she said.

"He cleaned yesterday, instead," Rose answered. "He doesn't always know his schedule in advance, so he's never sure just when he can get to the shop."

Addy continued to work with Rose on Wednesday afternoons, but she never saw Douglas there, and her mother didn't ask about him.

For several weeks, Rose was not particularly late getting home, but then, one Tuesday night, she was quite late again. Bess was angry by the time she came home.

"You're very late tonight, Rose. Addy and I are just about famished."

"Sorry, Mama. I set up a new display, and it took much longer than I thought it would. You two should start eating if I'm late. I don't mean you to wait."

"The display could have waited till tomorrow. You know I don't like you to be in the shop by yourself so late in the evening."

"The door was locked, Mama. And Douglas was cleaning, so I wasn't alone."

Bess glanced up in surprise and then returned to her meal with more concentration than Addy thought the soup required. When Bess looked up again, Rose was watching her. "I thought he cleaned on Wednesdays," Bess said.

"Not always," Rose responded. The expression on her face, just short of defiance, dared her mother to ask another question. Bess did not rise to the challenge.

"I don't mean to worry you, and I'll take more care not to be so late again," Rose said.

There's more to Rose than meets the eye, Addy thought. Still, she couldn't understand her mother's concern. Is it only the wagging tongues of busybodies that worry her, or does she think there is something between Rose and Douglas? Could Harriet be right? Rose and Douglas. Douglas kissing Rose, and Rose kissing Douglas. Rose as the woman Douglas loves and wants to marry and take home with him. Addy caught her breath. They'll leave me here alone with Mama.

Addy shook her head as if to clear it of such an absurd picture. Romance at Rose's age and with a much younger man like Douglas was ridiculous. Addy almost laughed out loud at the way she had let her imagination run away with her. The sight of Bess's stern face was enough, however, to quell any such outburst.

THE FIRST SUNDAY OF THE SUMMER BEFORE HIS LAST YEAR of medical school, Douglas suggested they all go for a walk from the palace to the castle along the Royal Mile. "There's just this year until I graduate, and I want you to help me have a lucky year."

"That's as good a reason as any for a lovely walk," Bess said, and the four of them set out for the palace.

When they reached the Heart of the Midlothian set in pavement at the former site of the Tollhouse Jail, Douglas stopped. "People spit on the medallion for good luck like they used to spit on the jailhouse doors," he said. "But you have to spit carefully so you don't miss the heart, because if you miss, it's bad luck instead of good luck."

"Look who's become a tour guide, showing us about our own city," Rose said. "And who told you this nonsense? I never did."

"Some of the medical students come here before their exams. They told me about it."

"So this is how you get your good grades," Rose said.

Douglas laughed. "You're on to me. This is, indeed, the secret of my success."

Everybody stood for a moment, looking at the medallion.

"Let's spit on it to bring ourselves good luck in the coming year," Douglas continued, smiling at Rose. "I know what I'm going to wish for."

"We'll do no such thing," Bess said. "It's foolish to tempt fate and trust your luck to an old wives' tale. And nobody in my household is going to be seen spitting on the ground in broad daylight."

As the others continued up the hill toward the castle, Addy lagged behind for an instant, closed her eyes in deep concentration, turned, and spit. She was pleased to see that she hit the heart, right in the middle.

A FEW DAYS LATER, DOUGLAS GOT A TELEGRAM. A TELEGRAM is never a good thing, and Bess left it on the table by the front door as if to bring it as little as possible into the house. She was knitting in the parlor when Douglas came in that evening. Rose had gone upstairs to get her book, and Addy was setting the kitchen table for breakfast.

"Do you need dinner?" Bess asked as he walked into the parlor.

"No, I ate with some other students at a pub."

"There's a telegram for you on the table by the front door," she said and went back to her knitting.

Douglas went to the foyer, and there was a long moment before he rejoined her. By then, Rose was also in the parlor, and Addy had stepped into the dining room and stood in the shadow of the breakfront.

"My father's sick and in the hospital," he said. "My mother wants me to come home." He looked at Rose and sat heavily in the chair opposite the sofa.

"What are you going to do?" Rose asked.

Douglas shook his head. He didn't speak immediately, and it wasn't clear to Addy what he might be about to say.

"Do as she asks," Bess said.

"Why should I?" Douglas got up and began to pace back and forth across the room. "He's a damn lousy father and a damn lousy husband, and he can die for all I care."

Addy was shocked by his harsh voice and crude language. She thought Rose looked shocked as well.

Bess didn't respond to his outburst or look up from her knitting. "That doesn't change your duty to your family."

"He never cared about his duty to us, so I don't see that I have any duty to him."

"It doesn't matter that you don't care about him. It's about what you owe your mother."

Douglas sat down and read the telegram again. "I can't go anyway. I don't have money for the passage."

"Don't worry about that. I'll advance your wages for cleaning the shop."

"You're helping me so much already. I can't ask you to do that."

"Don't be daft," Bess said. "I want to do it. I understand the worries of a woman with a sick husband. Your mother needs you now, and you need to go to her."

"Mama's right, Douglas," Rose said. "This is a time to set aside your feelings about your father and think about what your mother needs."

"I have lots of good reasons not to leave Scotland right now. I'm not sure my mother comes first before all of them."

Bess rested her knitting in her lap and looked at Douglas. "Your mother does come first before all of them," she said and picked up her knitting again. "I know there's your schooling and not wanting to fall behind the class, but I'm sure you can take leave and not miss so much that you won't graduate this year."

Douglas looked helplessly at Rose who said, "It's for you to decide, of course."

"It is," Douglas said and, after wishing them a curt goodnight, he went to his room.

Addy went upstairs to get the latest issue of *Amateur Gardening* from her bedroom. Poor Douglas, she thought, everybody is against him, even Rose. Why should mothers come first no matter what? It's a wonder that his mother thinks she can order him about from the other side of the ocean. I would have told him to stand strong and do just what he wants to do.

Addy sat on the edge of her bed and took off her shoes. She knew that once Douglas went to his room, house slippers wouldn't make her mother frown. It had been surprising to hear that Douglas was paid wages. Why aren't I paid wages? She reached under the bed for her slippers and pulled them on. What if he goes and doesn't come back? Maybe he'll feel safer on the other side of the Atlantic, far away from the Germans and their war. Or his mother might not let him return once she has him home again. And just when I'm finally old enough for parties and dances, he won't be here to introduce me to his friends."

Addy gathered up her magazine and joined her sister and her mother in the living room.

"What was Douglas's telegram about?" she asked.

"Nothing that concerns you," Bess answered.

Breakfast the next morning was a grim affair. Addy knew just what was on everybody's mind, and she knew that she wasn't supposed to know. It took all her willpower to wait and watch. It seemed to her that Bess and Rose were also bursting with questions they couldn't ask. Aside from offers of more toast and requests for more tea, there was no conversation.

Douglas went to his room for his satchel. When he came back through the kitchen, he said, "I've decided to take you up on your offer of an advance on my wages, and after I arrange a leave from school, I'll go home for a few weeks."

"You're doing the right thing, hard as it is," Bess said.

"I'm coming back as soon as I can."

The following Thursday, Douglas left for the States. Addy set only three places in the morning and at dinner and heard no more late-night tiptoeing across the kitchen. There was less laughter at breakfast, and chatting in the parlor in the evening lost its sparkle without the anecdotes Douglas brought from school.

"It doesn't seem like the whole family is here with Douglas gone," Bess said one morning. When neither Rose nor Addy responded, she continued, "Don't you think so, Rose?"

"Yes, I do."

"You seem disinclined to talk about it," Bess said. "Why are you so quiet?"

"There's nothing to talk about, and I'm thinking about all the things to be done before we open this morning. I think I'll get an early start." She left the table and rinsed her dishes at the sink.

"What's got you rushing off?" Addy asked.

"There's the mail to check and bills to pay," Rose said and left Addy and her mother sitting at the breakfast table.

Douglas must have missed them, too, because he wrote Bess a letter every few days. That's how Addy knew his father had tuberculosis and was transferred to a sanitarium close to home after two weeks in the hospital. The doctors expected him to recover. Bess also told them that Clara, Douglas's mother, and his two brothers and his sister were happy that he had found such a wonderful second home in Edinburgh.

Addy knew more than that, though, because she found Douglas's letters in her mother's room lying on the top of the dresser. She knew that Douglas's family speculated that his father had caught tuberculosis from his latest girlfriend, and none of the brothers cared if he recovered or not. It frustrated Douglas that his mother wouldn't admit to his father's gambling, drinking, and girlfriends, and even though the brothers openly disdained their father amongst themselves, Clara would not let them complain about him in front of her or their little sister.

Addy also found a note from Clara thanking Bess for opening her home to Douglas. She praised Bess's generosity and loving nature and congratulated her on having a brilliant businesswoman for an older daughter and a cute little housekeeper for a younger daughter. Addy was stung.

At the shop one afternoon, Addy put on a smock that Rose usually wore. In the pocket, she found an envelope that looked like an invoice and opened it to see if she was right. As she unfolded the letter, Addy recognized Douglas's handwriting, but before she could read what he had written, Rose came into the backroom.

"That's mine, Addy," Rose said, taking the letter from her.

Addy was suddenly ashamed of herself, though she felt no shame when she read the letters Douglas sent her mother. "Sorry, Rose. I was surprised to find an envelope in the pocket, and I looked to see what it was. I didn't read it."

"No harm done, Addy. Don't worry," Rose answered and put the letter in her purse.

Addy was annoyed that Douglas was writing to everybody but her and wondered if there were other letters to Rose and where they might be hidden.

ONE GLOOMY MORNING SEVERAL WEEKS AFTER DOUGLAS left, Rose woke with a headache and a stuffy nose and then added a cough.

"Just a nasty cold," Bess said and treated it with honey, lemon, and a spot of bourbon in hot tea.

Rose continued to go to the shop as usual but came home so tired she could only eat dinner before she went to bed. If

Bess wasn't worried, neither was Addy. Until she realized that Rose didn't have the energy to read before going to sleep.

When Rose's congestion and coughing worsened, Bess ordered her to stay home. "It won't do to have you coughing on the buttons and sneezing on the gloves," she said.

Rose acquiesced without an argument. She tried to do Addy's housework while Addy was at the shop, but Bess put a stop to that when it became clear that Rose could barely get herself dressed.

"We can manage the store and the house till you're on your feet again," she told Rose and, turning to Addy, added "There'll be no whining from you. We can't expect anything from Rose till she's better."

Bess needn't have warned Addy. By now, she was worried enough to do whatever was necessary to help Rose get well. That night, Addy woke suddenly to the sound of Rose coughing and was reminded of the last days of her father's illness. Could Rose be sick with the same thing? Addy hid under her blankets just as she had then and wondered if her mother was also hiding in her bed.

The next morning, Addy brought Rose her breakfast in bed.

"Thanks, Addy," Rose said, sipping her tea. "I love watching the garden from my window. I think I'll rest here for the day."

Bess would not hear of it and insisted on settling Rose on the couch, wrapped in a huge afghan Bess had knitted years before. Addy moved a little table near the couch for the radio and a pile of books and magazines. Only when Rose told them to stop fussing did they leave for the shop.

At first, they left Rose all day, but when they discovered that she slept right through lunch and didn't have anything to eat or drink until they came home in the evening, Bess came back in the middle of each day to be sure that Rose ate something for lunch and to set out a thermos of tea, a big cup, and a snack for her to have in the afternoon. Yet, in spite of their care, Rose's nasty cold was much worse by the end of the week.

The shop looked much worse, too. Although Bess and Addy were no busier than usual, they never found time to straighten the shelves or sort through the bins of things the customers mixed up during the day. It didn't help that Bess had spilled a new order of buttons on the floor in the backroom, and neither of them had had time to clean it up.

"I never realized before that there was so much stuff in this shop," Addy complained. "It always looked organized before. Why can't people put things they don't want back where they found them?"

Bess looked around and sighed. "We'll have to come in on Sunday and do nothing but set this place to rights."

It shocked and frightened Addy to see how incompetent a manager her mother proved to be. She missed Douglas, who certainly would have lent a helping hand in the crisis and whose growing expertise as a doctor would have been a comfort. And she missed Rose, who never would have let things get so out of hand in the first place.

Rose's condition did not improve, and she complained that her chest felt tight and it hurt to cough or take a deep breath. Addy didn't know which was more alarming, that Rose's symptoms were worsening or that she was complaining. I complain, Addy thought, not her.

When Rose developed a fever and had trouble catching her breath, Bess called the doctor. Addy suggested that they close the shop, but Bess sent her off alone and busied herself in the kitchen making a custard to tempt Rose to eat. It was the middle of the morning before the doctor arrived, and, still in her apron, Bess rushed from the kitchen to answer the door. She was relieved to see Dr. Fields, the elder, not his young son who had recently joined the practice.

"Dr. Fields, I'm glad to see you. It's Rose that's sick. She's here in the living room."

"Mrs. Kaminsky, always a pleasure. Let's have a look at the patient."

Bess hovered in the doorway while Dr. Fields examined Rose. He took her temperature, asked about her symptoms, and listened to her chest.

"Well, young lady," he said, patting Rose's hand, "my medical degree and years of experience tell me you are sick." Rose laughed, but Bess didn't. "It seems to me that you are taking care of yourself in just the right way. Now you need to be a patient patient and rest until you are well." Dr. Fields fitted his stethoscope into his medical bag. "I'll tell your mother a few details, but you are not to worry yourself about a thing. This is going around. It's stopped here, and it will stay a bit. So be a good lass, and get your rest and eat and drink what you can till it moves on."

Rose promised she would.

"May I offer you a cup of tea?" Bess asked.

Dr. Fields accepted and followed Bess to the kitchen. The two of them sat at the table, and after they had each had a sip of tea, Bess started to cry.

"Now, now, Mrs. Kaminsky, there's no need for tears."

"It's just like Joseph at the end," Bess sobbed.

"You're quite wrong there. It's not like Joseph at all. He was ill for a long, long time before he died of pneumonia. Rose is a young, healthy person, and she's going to get well. I do need you to keep an eye on her, and call me if you can't keep her fever down, but I'll not have you making more of this than it is. Don't you worry, and don't let Rose worry either."

After the doctor left, Bess took a cup of tea to Rose. "Dr. Fields says you are going to be fine, but this takes a bit of time to go away. Don't worry. It'll run its course in a day or two."

Addy came home that evening to find Rose sleeping and Bess in the kitchen setting soup bowls on trays. "You left me at the shop by myself," she grumbled. "I only had an apple for lunch, and I worried all day about why you didn't come. I was afraid you would be angry if I called."

"You're right about that. I would be angry if you called. The phone at the shop is only for business calls, and I was too busy here to be on the phone with you, anyway. I can't leave Rose, and I've no time to worry about your lunch." Bess turned back to the stove and stirred the soup. "You'll have to pack a lunch for the next few days and do the best you can at the shop. Now get ready for dinner."

Addy went to hang up her coat muttering to herself under her breath, "I may not be the daughter you carried out of Russia in your arms, but don't I matter just a little?"

Bess and Addy took trays into the living room and balanced them in their laps so they could be with Rose while they ate. Bess was happy that Rose drank a half cup of tea.

Addy told Rose about how Mrs. McAllister had come in looking for buttons for the bright green cardigan she's knitting and had loved the big gold buttons that Rose thought so gaudy she had almost left them off the order.

"There's not another shop that has these!" Mrs. McAllister had exclaimed.

Addy stood to demonstrate how she had solemnly responded, "We always have the most fashionable items here."

When Rose laughed and said, "You're a blessing with the customers," Addy smiled and went to get a napkin to replace the one that had slipped from Rose's lap to the floor. She didn't tell her sister or her mother that the shop was looking even messier, and that she had decided to go in early the next day to tidy up a bit.

That evening Bess helped Rose with a sponge bath and into a fresh nightie while Addy put fresh sheets on Rose's bed and dusted her room. When she got to the wooden box on the dresser, she noticed that the little golden key was not in the lock. Addy searched the top of the dresser and the floor around it, but she couldn't find the key. She didn't want Rose to worry, so she didn't tell her that the key was missing.

Bess kissed Rose on her forehead, and Addy patted her sister's hand before they left the room.

"We'll leave the door open," Bess said. "Just call if you need anything."

"Don't worry, Mama," Rose said. "All I need is a bit of a rest. Washing up wore me out."

Addy stayed upstairs and got ready for bed. She left her bedroom door ajar in case Rose called and was already under the covers when she heard her mother come up the stairs. Bess stopped at Rose's doorway, and Addy could hear her mother crying. Then she heard her mother whisper, "I can't lose her." It was quiet for a moment until Bess broke out anew, "Rose," she sobbed quietly, "It's you I can't do without. Don't leave me, Rose. Don't leave me."

Addy was alarmed at her mother's outburst. Even when her father had stayed in bed all day and coughed all night, her mother never stood outside his room crying. Is this worse than that was? Addy sat up and found herself gasping for breath. Rose has to get well. I can't be left alone here with Mother.

Addy swung her legs out of bed as her mother walked past her bedroom door. What if Rose was awake and had heard everything? What if Rose thinks she's dying? When Bess was safely in her own room, Addy tiptoed to Rose's doorway and listened for a moment. She thought she heard a muffled sound and hurried to the bed. Rose looked up.

"Rose," Addy whispered. "You're awake. How are you feeling? Did you hear Mama…tell you goodnight?"

"I heard her," Rose said and started to cry.

"Rose, don't let her make you sad." Addy sat on the edge of the bed and took her sister's hand. "You're going to be fine. You know Mama always worries more than she needs to about everything."

"She said she can't do without me."

"Well, she won't have to, will she? You aren't dying, Rose, so you aren't going anywhere. Dr. Fields said you are going to be better in just a few days. Please don't worry. None of us is supposed to worry, especially you."

It was some time before Rose stopped crying. Addy stayed at her bedside, patting her hand, until she finally became quiet.

"You'll be up and about in no time, Rose, and nothing will be changed."

"Everything is changed," Rose said.

"No, you'll see. It will all be fine."

"What am I going to do? I've been so foolish."

"Rose, don't be silly. You didn't choose to be sick. You're never foolish," Addy hesitated and then added, "…except now when you say you've been foolish, of course."

Rose laughed, and Addy felt pleased to have cheered her up. "Now go to sleep," she said.

"You're a good sister, Addy. Now you go to bed, too. You must be exhausted, yourself."

Bess sent Addy off to the shop by herself and stayed home to care for Rose. On the third day, Dr. Fields was back in the house.

"You're doing everything right, Mrs. Kaminsky," he reassured Bess. "Keep her fever down, and don't let her see you worry."

When Addy came home late that afternoon, she found Rose sleeping on the couch and Bess asleep in the big winged chair with her book of psalms in her lap. Addy knew this was the one thing Bess's mother had given her when she left Russia. Bess must have been reading it next to Rose until she fell asleep, herself. Addy stood in the doorway and watched the two of them. She was surprised at how small and old her mother looked.

Addy went to the kitchen and was warming the soup from the night before when her mother came in.

"Addy, stop making so much noise. You'll wake Rose," she whispered.

"Is she better today?" Addy asked.

"Of course she's better. It was always just a matter of time."

And, indeed, Rose was better. She even ate a little soup and said it was delicious.

That evening Addy asked Rose if she would like a book from her room, but Rose said she was too tired to read.

"I remember when you used to read to me, Rose," Addy said. "My favorite story was about Rose Red and Snow White, and I made you read it every day. I knew you must be Rose Red, so I must be Snow White." Addy laughed. "And I remember that when you were already much too old for dolls, you still played dolls with me. You even agreed to be the mother of the doll whose arm was ripped a little, so I could be the mother of the doll with the curly yellow hair."

"I liked the old doll better, Addy. I wasn't doing you a favor."

"And you would never let the boy doll boss you around

even though I said he was the husband. So I had to be his wife, until you told me we could do without him altogether."

"Oh dear, Addy. I didn't know I was such a bad influence on you." Rose laughed, but then began to cough.

Bess jumped up from her chair in alarm. "Enough of your silly stories, Addy. Now you've got her coughing."

Rose sipped the tea Bess handed her and took a breath. "Don't blame Addy, Mama. Talking and laughing helps me know that I'm getting well, after all." She laid back on the couch. "You're good for me, Addy."

Addy smiled and made the afghan more snug around Rose's feet.

THE NEXT EVENING, ROSE SAID, "LET'S START YOUR READING life, Addy. Since you liked Rose Red and Snow White so much, we could read another story about sisters."

Addy agreed and was sent upstairs to get *The Woman in White* from Rose's book shelf. Rose propped the book on her knees and began to read, but her breath quickly gave out.

"Here, Rose. Give it to me. It's too big and heavy for you to hold up like that. Let me read to you." Addy took the book, and Rose settled back on the couch.

Every evening after dinner, Addy read to Rose. Bess also listened to the story while she knitted.

Addy loved the spooky beginning, and Rose's little picture of a ghost-like woman in the margin. "Seeing your little pictures of the characters is the best part of reading a book you've already read, Rose."

After that, Addy had to pass the book to her mother every time there was a picture in the margin so that Bess could enjoy

Rose's miniature portraits, too.

Addy could not contain her surprise when Walter met Laura with Marian in the graveyard. "I thought she was dead!" she said and turned to her mother. "Didn't you think she was dead?"

"I did, Addy. I'm just as shocked as you are. You did a fine job of not telling us, Rose."

"I wanted you to be as surprised as I was the first time I read this book," Rose said.

"You're just like Marian, Rose. You're strong and sensible, and you can hold your tongue. I'm like Laura, helpless and useless," Addy said.

"Don't be silly, Addy. You're just as strong and sensible as I am," Rose said.

But Addy wasn't so sure, and she thought her mother looked unconvinced.

"I never could be like Marian," Addy said. "Look at the way she gives up Walter. Like it's her duty."

"I don't think Marian sees it as a sacrifice. Sometimes a person's duty is also their preference," Rose responded.

"I don't understand that," Addy said, and Rose did not try to explain further.

By the end of the book, Rose was nearly well enough to return to the shop. She agreed to another week of rest and a fortnight of half days, before resuming her old schedule.

ON THE MORNING BEFORE ROSE WAS SCHEDULED TO return to the shop, Bess followed Addy to the front door. "I can only imagine how much worse the shop must look since you've been there by yourself, Addy. Close at noon today, and spend as long as it takes to clean up. We can't have Rose greeted by a mess tomorrow and think she's the one expected to fix it."

Addy spent the afternoon and the early evening cleaning the shop. She stacked the ribbon on the shelves behind the counter, filled the bins with spools of thread, and displayed the cards of buttons on the counter top. She hung the blouses carefully from their rods and arranged the gloves in their glass display cases. She even cleaned the storeroom and swept and mopped the floor.

A good part of the afternoon was spent on her hands and knees hunting for the buttons her mother had spilled weeks before. You can't blame this on me, Addy thought, as she reached under Rose's work table in search of buttons. As if you had nothing to do with it. Who spilled all the buttons, after all? And how do you know the shop isn't looking better than the last time you were here? And why do you think that I need to be told to clean up for Rose? That last instruction made Addy angriest of all. The transformation of the shop was going to be her surprise, her special gift to Rose. Now her mother would see it as nothing more than following directions.

The next morning, Addy proudly led Rose and Bess into the shop and waited for their comments. "Isn't it looking pretty?" Addy said. "And don't you think the little vase of flowers on the counter adds a nice touch?"

Rose looked around like a mother might look at her only child dressed funny by the sitter after his nap.

"Addy did the best she could," Bess said, "but I'm sure you'll agree that the shop needs you."

Rose nodded and said, "Thank you, Addy, for taking such good care of the shop while I was sick."

Though Rose only worked half days at first, the shop soon became efficient and comfortable again. The merchandise looked inviting in the displays she created and the stock, though plentiful as usual, did not seem in disarray. Rose also hired a girl, Annie, to come in after school to dust and mop and straighten up. It made Addy feel quite grown up to laugh with Bess and Rose at Annie's funny stories about her teachers and her classmates.

"Addy and I did our best, but there's nobody like you for running the shop, Rose," Bess said on more than one occasion. "You're your father's daughter, after all."

Rose was resting after her first full day at the shop when she saw Addy pass by her bedroom doorway. "Addy," she called out, "thank you for taking such good care of me when I was sick. Come, sit here," she added, patting the edge of her bed.

Addy was happy to comply. "You've thanked me enough, Rose. I knew you would get better, but Mama was very worried. Even now that you're better, she still seems worried about losing you."

"She's not going to lose me, and I need to make that clearer."

"Don't go rushing your recovery, Rose. Dr. Fields warned us about letting you do too much."

"Don't worry. I'm careful to rest like a good girl every afternoon before dinner."

Addy felt quite grown up talking like this with Rose. She glanced around the room and saw the bookshelves. "It was fun reading *The Woman in White* with you. I think I'll start borrowing books you've already read, if that's alright."

"Of course. I already invited you to." Rose smiled. "I see my illness turned you into a reader, Addy," she teased. "Maybe that's why I got sick."

"I hope not," Addy said, pleased be sharing a joke with Rose. "What book do you suggest?"

"What did you like about *The Woman in White*?"

"That it was about sisters, and I liked the mystery."

"Then try one of my mysteries next. We'll build up to more weighty novels."

Just then they heard Bess calling from the front door, "Addy, get down here and help me with these parcels."

Addy gave Rose a little hug and rushed downstairs to help her mother.

As she dusted Rose's room the next morning, Addy was relieved to see the little key back in the lock of Rose's wooden box. Perhaps it hadn't been lost after all. Rose might have put it someplace for safe keeping. She carefully turned it to look inside. The box was full of silk scarves, as usual.

When she finished cleaning, Addy scanned the titles on Rose's bookshelves looking for a mystery. It's hard to tell what a book is about from a title, she thought, and finally took *Crime and Punishment* off the shelf and put it in her room.

Slowly, life resumed its familiar pattern. Rose grew stronger and worked until closing every day at the shop. Addy kept house in the morning and went to the shop in the afternoon so Rose could do the bookkeeping and set up displays without having to stay late.

Bess took the longest to recover. She spent more time in the morning muttering to herself in her room, until Addy worried that Rose's illness had changed her mother. But eventually Addy saw, with both relief and regret, that Bess was becoming her old self again. If anything, she was more vigilant and intrusive than before and made sure to know just where Addy was each minute of the day. She even kept closer track of Rose.

Every day, Bess came home early from the shop and took responsibility for the evening meal. Addy noticed that dinner always included some delicacy or one of Rose's favorite foods, like noodle pudding with raisins and cottage cheese or custard perfectly baked with a sprinkle of nutmeg on top. Addy wasn't sorry to see her mother catering to Rose, but she wondered if Bess would have been so solicitous if she had been the one to get sick.

In the evening, the three women sat in the living room listening to the radio. Sometimes Addy read, and sometimes she planned her fall garden; Rose always read, in spite of the radio in the background. Bess was knitting a new shawl for Rose to use at the shop when the weather turned chilly. It was a soft heather white with a lavender thistle pattern. Addy knew that white heather was supposed to have magical properties and wondered what magic spell her mother hoped this shawl would produce

For the most part, it was a peaceful time; only the news from Europe could dispel the quiet mood. Bess would sigh whenever broadcasts from Germany came on, and her knitting needles would click at a ferocious pace until she would stop suddenly and rest them in her lap. When the needles ceased, Rose would look up and study her mother until Bess picked up her knitting again. Then Rose would return to her book. Addy wished they would turn off the radio and leave the Germans to themselves. Why bring them and their vulgar noise into a quiet parlor in Edinburgh? Once Addy caught Bess studying each of her daughters in turn as if she were choosing melons at the grocers. Addy half-expected her mother to sniff their hair and thump their foreheads, listening for a hollow sound.

Bess no longer shared news of Douglas, and there were no letters on her dresser either. As curious as she was, Addy didn't want to ripple the calm in the household by asking about him. It doesn't matter if he comes back or not, she reasoned. Soon I'll be going to dances and meeting boys as easily without him in the house as with him here. They'll line up to dance with me, and they'll beg to see me home. Tall boys and blond boys and handsome boys with lovely smiles. They'll all fancy me, but I'll fancy just one of them, the best one. All the girls will want to dance with him, but he'll only want to dance with me and marry me and take me home with him. I can make that happen without any help from anyone.

⫸⫸⫶⫷⫷

WHEN DOUGLAS ARRIVED AT BREAKFAST TIME THREE WEEKS later, Addy was astonished by the change in him. He was thinner, his hair was shorter, and he had shaved his moustache. His thin upper lip accentuated his long, thin nose and gave him a miserly appearance. She didn't like it.

"Douglas!" Bess said, looking him over with an appraising eye. "What an odd time to get back."

Douglas looked unsettled by her greeting. "I got in late last night, and I was afraid I would frighten everybody by coming in the back door at such an hour. So I stayed one night on a friend's couch." When no one responded, he continued, "I'll just put my bag in my room. Breakfast looks good."

When he returned to the kitchen, he was holding three packages. "I brought something from the States for each of you. My brother's girlfriend helped me pick them out. Except this one for Rose," he said, giving her a big square package. He gave Bess a small square box and Addy a long thin one.

"Aren't you going to open your presents?" he asked. "It was fun to buy them, but it's much more fun to see you open them."

Bess opened her gift first and found a silver pin in the shape of country cottage. "What a lovely brooch," she said, holding it up for all to see. "You didn't need to buy me anything, but it is very nice that you did."

Rose's package was the biggest and the heaviest, and when she opened it, she found a book. "*Gone with the Wind*," she said. "I haven't heard of it."

"It's all the rage in the States," Douglas said. "They say it will surely win prizes. I hope you like it."

"I'm sure I will," Rose said and smiled at him.

When Addy opened her gift, she found a sheer silk scarf. It was a pale, creamy color with lilacs sprinkled across it. "Douglas, thank you! It's beautiful," she exclaimed and wrapped the scarf around her neck. "The flowers look so real, I can almost smell them, and it will be perfect with my new dress."

"It looks very nice on you. Even over your sweater and apron. I'm glad you like it." Douglas looked around the table. "I missed you all. It was lonely on the ship by myself. I don't ever want to make that trip alone again." Douglas smiled at Rose, who looked down at her plate. Douglas's smiled faded, and he turned his attention to the eggs Addy put at his place.

"There must have been a problem with the mail," he continued, "because I didn't get any letters after the first couple of weeks."

"We were very busy, Douglas," Bess said. "And we're still busy, so it's time we left for the shop." She got up from the table, and Douglas got up when she did.

"I'd like to hear about how you all are, but I suppose I'd better go to school and let them know I'm back," he said. "Maybe I'll come by the shop later to mop up."

"We hired a girl to help," Bess said. "For now, I don't want you to worry about anything but your studies."

Douglas watched her and Rose leave the kitchen before he went for his coat and satchel. They left the house before he reappeared.

"Are you all happy to see me, Addy?" he asked as he came back into the kitchen.

"Of course," Addy said, but she wasn't sure it was true. Her mother didn't seem happy to see him, and Rose hadn't smiled at him except when she thanked him for the book. And a book could always make Rose smile.

"Is everything all right here? Your mother said Rose was sick in the last letter she sent me, but it didn't sound serious."

Addy wondered why her mother hadn't written Douglas the truth about Rose's illness. Maybe it was because he was too far away to do anything but worry. If so, there was no reason not to tell the truth now.

"It was very serious, and she had to stay home for more than three weeks. Mama and I tried to keep the shop going by ourselves, but we weren't very good at it. Now that Rose is well, everything is fine again."

"Why didn't your mother tell me the truth?"

"Probably because you had your own family problems to worry about," Addy said. "How is your father?" she quickly added and wondered why none of them had thought to ask before.

"He's expected to get better." Douglas looked around the kitchen for a moment. "My mother can't wait till I finish school and come home for good, but sometimes I think I'd rather stay here forever."

"You can't do that if your family needs you."

Douglas nodded. "I know, but I'm surprised you feel that way."

"Oh, it doesn't apply to me. Since I am quite unnecessary, I can do whatever I want."

"How can you say that?" Douglas said. "You know we all need you. We would starve in the morning if not for you."

N.R. King

"That's a load of blarney and you know it. Anyone can stir porridge." Addy laughed and turned her attention to the dishes. I am glad to see him, she thought. Now that he's back, I'm glad he's back.

THE FAMILY RARELY SAW DOUGLAS EXCEPT AT BREAKFAST. Sometimes on Sunday, he would say that he had a few hours to relax and ask Rose to visit a park or a museum with him, but she always said she was busy or tired. Addy worried that Rose might be getting sick again.

The second Sunday he was back, Douglas suggested that he and Rose make dinner like they used to. Before Rose could respond, Bess pointed out that he must have studying to do and the family shouldn't intrude on his time. She suggested that Rose and Addy cook together, instead. Addy was thrilled when Rose seconded the suggestion, saying, "I would love to fix dinner with Addy. She's such a good cook, I'm sure to learn something from her."

"Just like I learn from you in the shop," Addy said. "Though I don't really think I have anything to teach you in the kitchen," she added quickly, fearing she might have seemed boastful.

"You don't believe that, Addy. You know good cooking is an art, and in the kitchen, you are the artist," Rose said.

Addy grinned and hurried into the kitchen to find a fresh apron for Rose. Only Douglas looked disappointed when he was banished to his room to study and wait to be called for dinner.

Later that week, Bess finished the shawl she was knitting for Rose and presented it to her one evening after dinner. Rose wrapped it around herself and pulled it high over her shoulders. "I've never felt so safe from the cold…so safe from everything," she said. "Thank you."

Addy had never seen such a lovely, soft wrap. The thistle pattern was delicately woven into the white heather background, making the shawl look like an impregnable hedge. When Rose wore it, she seemed to disappear within its folds.

Bess smiled broadly. "You'll have to decide if you want to keep it at the shop or at home," she said.

"For now, I'm going to keep it here," Rose answered. "When the weather gets cold, I may carry it back and forth with me every day so I'm never without it."

"I might have to make another one so you have one wherever you go," Bess said.

Rose laughed as if her mother were joking, but Addy wasn't sure.

Knitting for her daughters was something Bess had done all their lives. It was less characteristic behavior when, later that week, Bess gave Rose a book.

"Have you read this?" Bess asked. "It's just won the big prize for fiction, and I'm told the story is about an extraordinary woman."

"I haven't read it," Rose said, "but I've heard that it's a fine book."

Addy could see the cover and the title, *South Riding*. "I haven't even heard of it," she said.

"I wouldn't expect you to have heard of it," Bess said.

"I'll read it next, and then lend it to you, Addy," Rose said. "Thanks, Mama. It's very kind of you to look out for the latest books." Rose gave her mother a kiss on her cheek. "You take good care of me, and don't think that I don't notice."

Addy thought her mother's eyes looked suddenly moist and knew better than to comment.

N.R. King

THE FOLLOWING SUNDAY AFTERNOON, ADDY OVERHEARD Rose and Douglas talking in the foyer.

"Rose, this is Scotland. It's always raining or about to rain or just over raining. You won't get wet in a little bit of drizzle so put on your hat and coat and let's go out. I haven't long before my next shift at the hospital, and I want to talk to you."

"I can't worry Mother. Since I've been sick, she's concerned about my health."

"Why didn't you tell me how sick you were?"

"It wasn't necessary to worry you. I knew I would get well. And I did write you a letter after I was strong again."

"We need to talk about that letter."

"On the contrary, my letter spoke for itself."

"But it must be obvious that I don't accept anything it said. How could you make such an important decision when I was gone?"

"That's when everything became clear."

Bess suddenly left her bedroom with a great clatter and appeared at the top stairs. Addy had just enough time to scurry along the hallway and into the parlor.

"Oh, Douglas," Bess said, "I thought you were going out."

"I just stopped for a moment's conversation with Rose. We'll talk again, Rose."

Douglas let himself out, and Rose and Bess went into the parlor where they found Addy going through the pages of *The Treasure Book of Fairytales*.

"It's been a long time since you've had that off the shelf," Rose said. "I remember when you decided to keep your scraps in its pages. Are they still there?"

"They are," said Addy and held up several small, glossy pictures of flowers and princesses and animal babies. "I was wondering if I should throw them out now that I'm older."

"Don't do that," Rose said. "It's a comfort sometimes to look over things from long ago."

"I remember when Daddy came home from the shop with a page of these as a surprise," Addy said, holding up a duckling wearing a jaunty blue cap. She looked over a page of baskets filled with large blooms and another of lords and ladies in fancy dress. "You're right, Rose. I should save them."

ROSE WAITED UNTIL SHE HAD FINISHED *GONE WITH THE Wind* before she brought it up at breakfast.

"Did you like it?" Douglas asked.

"I did. It was full of adventure and fascinating characters."

"Didn't you think Scarlett was brave and daring?"

"How do you know about Scarlett? Did you read the book?"

"It was a long voyage, Rose. I had lots of time on the boat, and I did read the book before I got here. I was very careful, and you must admit that you didn't guess."

"That's true enough. And I did like Scarlett. But I liked her best when she was true to what she was raised to be. I liked her best when she returned home to Tara."

"But what about Rhett? Don't you think she should have been better to him?"

There was an intensity to Douglas's question that silenced Bess and Addy.

"There was only Tara for Scarlett. There was Tara at the beginning, and there was Tara at the end. If she had realized that sooner, she would have saved herself a lot of heartache in the middle. It made it interesting for the reader, of course, but Scarlett should have been able to grow up without all that drama."

"But when she goes back to Tara at the end, she has nothing."

"How can you say that, Douglas? She has the land she's attached to, and she has her independence. She has everything she needs, and she'll realize it as soon as she gets home."

"You don't mean that."

"I do. I really do."

"But what about Rhett?"

"Don't worry about him. He'll be fine."

"Will they be friends?"

"Of course, they'll be friends."

"Will that make her happy?"

"That's exactly what will make her happy. And if she's happy, he'll be happy, too."

It wasn't clear that Douglas agreed, but he made no further comment.

As soon as everybody was out of the house, Addy made herself another cup of tea and sat at the kitchen table with it. Everything is the same and everything is different, she thought. Having Douglas back makes that obvious, and even though he doesn't know it yet, he'll figure it out. He'll see how Mother is suddenly old, and Rose is suddenly quiet and I am suddenly grown up.

Later, when Douglas had, indeed, figured it out, he also became suddenly old and suddenly quiet and suddenly grown up. By then, Addy wasn't thinking about him anymore. She was thinking about the dances in the fall.

Dangerous Boys

1936

ADDY WAS A GREAT ONE FOR FAVORITES. SHE HAD A FAVORite room, the kitchen; a favorite tree, the old apple tree in the garden; a favorite color, pink when she was little, lavender now; and a favorite person, Rose. Sometimes she wondered if Rose had favorites, too, and what they might be. The shop, of course, would be Rose's favorite place, and books would be Rose's favorite things. But who would be Rose's favorite person? Addy hoped she was.

Addy also had a favorite meal, breakfast, because then Rose would share what she had read the night before, and everybody would speculate about what might happen next. Ever since she began reading her way through Rose's collection of favorite books, Addy had been an eager participant.

"Why did you choose *Crime and Punishment*?" Rose had asked the first time she noticed that Addy had borrowed a book.

"You said to choose a mystery, so I did."

"Maybe you should begin with something a little easier."

"I don't need something easier."

"Don't be insulted, Addy. I just want to get your reading life off to a good start."

"No need to worry about me. This will be a good start," Addy had said, and, even though it took a long time, she surprised her mother and Rose, one morning, with the news that she had finished *Crime and Punishment*.

"But it wasn't really a mystery," she complained, "since I knew right away who did it." She couldn't understand why Rose looked amused since *Crime and Punishment* was anything but a funny book.

"Did you like it even though it wasn't what you expected?" Rose asked.

"I did like it, but it was hard to keep track of the people because their names were so strange, and sometimes they used different names, altogether. Mostly I loved your little portraits along the sides of the pages." Addy took another piece of toast and spread jelly on it. "Imagine doing something so terrible that you weren't like normal people any more. I didn't know till the end if he would confess."

"Did you think he was a good man?"

"How could he be a good man? He killed that old lady on purpose for no good reason. But his mother was worse." She looked up to see Rose frown and glance at Bess with concern. Addy instantly regretted bringing up the mother.

"What was so bad about the mother?" Bess asked.

"I didn't mean she was worse," Addy said. "I meant that things were worse for her. She had a lot of troubles and problems with everything that went on." Confident that her mother would not read the book, Addy added, "Her son caused her some heartache, and it was really sad for her."

Rose nodded and smiled at her in what Addy thought was an approving way. So she was glad she hadn't mentioned that she thought it terrible the way the mother was always sacrificing her daughter to take care of her son, and even telling herself that she was doing a good thing. At least the murderer never told himself that. What kind of mother throws away one child to take care of the other one?

"Boys are a bother," Addy said to Rose. "It's good we don't have a brother!"

Rose had laughed, and then reminded Addy that they had planned to read books together. Since then, to Addy's delight, they had read book after book about sisters.

Some mornings their mother talked about what she had read in the newspaper or heard on the radio. These were somber mornings because of the news from Europe. Once, Addy was shocked to see her mother begin to cry as her fears overwhelmed her.

"I don't know what I'll do if that madman, Hitler, comes here. I promised your father I would keep you safe and protect the shop. But how can I get you to safety and still save the shop? What can I do against armies?"

Before either of her daughters could react, Bess had dried her eyes and regained her composure, saying "That's enough of my silliness."

ADDY ALSO HAD A FAVORITE DAY OF THE YEAR, HER BIRTHDAY, and a favorite birthday, her nineteenth. That was how old she needed to be before her mother would let her go to the dances the local Jewish community sponsored for the Jewish medical students. All of the girls Addy knew hoped to marry medical students from the States and cross the ocean as the wives of young doctors. Addy was no exception. But, as excited as she was about the dances in the fall, she had been careful to keep her excitement to herself. There was no sense in bringing them up too soon. Now, with her birthday just days away, she began planning.

Perhaps dinner on the day after her nineteenth birthday would be best. Her mother would see that she was thinking about the fall dances but was restrained enough to have made no mention of them on her birthday, itself. Maybe by dinner the next day, somebody else would already have mentioned the dances and praised her self-control and maturity. But even if she had to bring up the topic herself, dinner was still a good choice. Rose would be there, and her mother was less likely to put her off if there was an audience. And, if need be, an older sister might become a valuable ally.

On the other hand, waiting all the way to dinner might not be a good idea. Her mother and Rose might be tired after a day in the shop, and her mother might be in a difficult mood. Maybe breakfast would be best. A lovely breakfast to catch her mother before she saw the newspaper and launched into a tirade about the Nazi threat, before some customer spilled all the spools of ribbon reaching for the green one at the back when there was a perfectly good green one in the front, before her mother got a headache. If she was lucky, Douglas might even sit a minute and have a cup of tea before he rushed out to class. Her mother was much nicer with Douglas around.

Addy's birthday arrived, at last, and her mother and Rose celebrated with roast beef for dinner and a chocolate layer cake for dessert. They each gave her a gift: a warm, lavender scarf fringed in white from her mother and a beautiful pearl brooch and a book, *Howards End*, from Rose.

"A book about sisters," Rose said. "I've read it, and I'm anxious to hear what you think of the story. Let me know when you finish, and we can talk about it."

Just what she might have said to one of her friends, Addy thought, and that was the best gift of all.

All through dinner and the evening, Addy was careful to let no mention of the significance of this birthday or the upcoming dances pass her lips. Nobody else mentioned the dances, either. The next morning, she woke ready to launch her plan.

Addy began by fixing her mother's favorite breakfast, kippers and eggs with crispy toast and hot, hot tea. The sizzle of the kippers in the frying pan and the warm fragrance of the eggs brought Rose to the table a little earlier than usual, and Addy was pleased when Douglas also sat down with them, saying, "This breakfast is too good to pass up even if I have to run to my first class." As soon as everybody was eating, Addy began.

"The Young Jewish Society is having dances again this year."

"Of course, they are," her mother said. "They have dances every year."

"It's just sixpence a head."

"Just like every year."

"But this year I'm nineteen. This is the year you said I could go to the dances."

"I know what I said, Addy. You don't need to remind me. Who else is going?"

"We're all going. The whole group. Iris has been going to dances since last year. She'll be there and Rita and her sister, Melinda, and Eileen, and Harriet, and one or two others. We're all old enough now."

"Melinda is only eighteen."

"Her mother said she can go as long as her sister is there."

"An excellent idea. Maybe Rose should go with you."

"It's fine with me if Rose wants to go," Addy said, pleased that permission had been so easily secured and confident that Rose would not want to go. It must have been the combination of kippers and Douglas.

Several days later, Bess brought up the subject again at breakfast. "The first dance of the year is in two weeks."

Addy was surprised her mother was so well informed and feared her permission to attend was about to be rescinded. The moment was too dangerous to risk a comment without more information. She nodded and was relieved when her mother continued.

"Rose, are you planning to go?"

"No, I wasn't planning on it," Rose said.

"Would you go with Addy as a favor to me?"

"I don't mind going along," Rose said.

Addy was grateful. Still, she didn't like the idea of showing up at her first dance with a sister who was eight years her senior and would be the oldest person in the room.

"I don't need Rose to chaperone me," Addy said. "I know how to take care of myself. These aren't dangerous boys." But even as she spoke, she knew that wasn't true. These were dangerous boys. A boy might behave like a suitor until his graduation and then return home without the girlfriend who thought she would be going with him as his wife. Everybody could name several such cases, and Addy knew she had to be careful.

"I don't plan on playing the part of chaperone. I'll just be there," Rose replied.

"I'll go, too," Douglas said from the kitchen doorway. Addy was not the only one who looked at him in surprise. In all the years he had been boarding with them, they had not known him to go to a dance.

"That would be nice of you, Douglas," Bess said, after a moment.

"My pleasure," he said and grinned at Rose as he took a piece of toast and hurried out the door. Addy wondered if he was going because she would be there or because Rose would be there or for some other reason, altogether.

Bess didn't object when Addy pointed out that she needed a new dress for the dance, and she didn't object when she saw the price. The dress was the same pale lavender as the flowers on the silk scarf Douglas had given her after his trip to the States months before, and Addy planned to wear the scarf with it. She wondered if Douglas would notice.

The night of the dance, Addy dressed carefully and was ready well before time to leave the house. She didn't want to seem overeager, so she stood quietly in her room, fearful that her dress might wrinkle if she sat down, and waited to be called. She could hear Rose opening and closing drawers, and she felt a little sorry that her sister had to go to the dance. She was sure that Rose would rather stay at home, or go to a movie with her friends.

Rose went downstairs, and her voice reached Addy from the foyer. "I thought Addy was down here already, Douglas. She started dressing hours ago." Then Rose called out, "Addy, are you ready?" Only then did Addy descend the stairs, pleased with Douglas's look of surprise and admiration.

"Addy, it seems to me that you grew up overnight," he said.

"How do I look?" she asked, enjoying the effect she was having on him.

"In a word, beautiful."

"Do you notice anything in particular?"

"Yes, we do," Rose said. "You're wearing the pretty scarf Douglas brought you from the States. It's perfect with the dress. Turn so I can see the back."

Rose watched Addy make two pirouettes across the foyer. "You've lovely taste, Addy, and you wear your clothes like royalty. Don't you agree, Douglas?"

"I couldn't agree more."

Addy tried to walk sedately with a gracious smile on her lips, as if going to a dance was the most ordinary thing in the world to be doing. Her composure would last a few minutes before her excitement boiled over in a rush of good spirits and babble, and she would have to remind herself to behave like an adult. Each new resolution failed, and in no time she was all aflutter again.

Rose was indulgent toward Addy and amused by Douglas as he squired the two of them along the sidewalk. His demeanor made Rose laugh. "Douglas, you look ready to defend our honor at a moment's notice," she said.

Douglas laughed. "I take my responsibility as the guardian of two charming ladies seriously."

"Quite unnecessary," Rose assured him. "Just feel like a friend, and I'll be the guardian of both of you. Who knows who will have their eyes on you? You're each a fine catch. Even though Addy is a silly, young thing, she can cook. And even though you are a serious, old thing, you are smart, and you are almost a doctor."

"I am not a silly, young thing," Addy said.

"And I'm not old," Douglas said.

"Given the present company, I guess that's true," Rose said. "We'll be old together tonight."

"Don't worry, Rose, we won't be the oldest in the room. Most of the Jewish students come to this dance to look over the fresh crop of girls, and the girls come to look over the students. It's a bit frantic, Addy. The parties later in the year are nicer."

Addy wondered how he knew that. It had always seemed that Douglas didn't go to parties or out with girls. It was intriguing to think he might have a secret life they knew nothing about. Maybe he's been to every dance since he started medical school. Does he dance with every girl in the room, or does he choose one favorite and lure her into a dark corner? And what about parties? What goes on at parties?

When they arrived at the dance, Addy rushed off to join her friends. Everything delighted her—the room, the decorations, the drinks, the music, and most of all, the boys. At last, a little crowd of boys approached their group, and every girl had a partner for the next dance. That was the last Addy saw of her friends for the rest of the evening.

The hours of practicing in Harriet's living room paid off. Addy was a little surprised and very pleased to realize that she was one of the best dancers in the room, especially sought out for the Lindy and the quick step. The precise, intricate footwork of the quick step appealed to her. Many others looked clumsy trying to put it together, but Addy knew she looked good. Some of the American boys hadn't seen the quick step before, and then it was her turn to play teacher.

Addy learned a new dance too, truckin', and it became her favorite. She watched once, focusing on a tall redhead wearing a green spangly dress. The next time the dance came around, Addy was also shuffling across the room, winking at her partner, wagging her index finger in the air, and arranging her mouth in the same mischievous smile she'd seen on the redhead.

After a hectic Lindy, Addy's partner bowed with a flourish, led her to a table, and offered to get her a drink. "Lemonade, please," she said, in accordance with her mother's direction to drink only lemonade and to be sure it had a pure flavor. Addy didn't want Rose to be put in a difficult position.

"I just love your accent. It's so soft and sweet," he said and went off to get her drink.

Addy watched him walk away. He was certainly good-looking with his glossy dark hair and his bright smile. When he disappeared in the crowd, she looked around. The dance floor was filled with couples, and all the chairs along the walls and around the tables were occupied. Rose and Douglas were sitting at a table across the room, their heads close together so they could hear each other over the music. Addy saw Rose reach out and rest her hand on his as Douglas threw his head back in laughter. What had Rose said that amused him? Addy watched as they sat there for a moment with their hands touching before he leaned toward her and said something that made Rose laugh. Addy hadn't seen her sister so flushed and high-spirited before, or Douglas so relaxed. He made no move to dance, and he didn't look frustrated to be sitting with somebody as old and plain as Rose. What could they be talking about?

Just then a cold glass of lemonade was thrust at her. "Here's your drink, m'lady," said her partner, and he sat down in the chair next to hers. "My name's Aaron, by the way, and I guess you can tell from my accent that I'm a long way from home."

Addy took one last look at Douglas and Rose and turned her attention to Aaron. "I'm Addy."

"You're a terrific dancer. Where did you learn?" Aaron said.

"Oh, I've been dancing for a long time," Addy replied. "I took dance lessons for several years when I was younger, and every time I come to a dance, I learn something new. You're quite good, yourself."

"Thanks. My sister taught me in our living room. She said I needed more than book learning to be a success at medical school. She's back in New Jersey, and the next time I write home, I'll have to say that her lessons helped me meet the prettiest girl and the best dancer at my very first dance."

"You've a way with your tongue as well as your feet," Addy said, and flashed him the smile she had practiced with Harriet until their cheeks hurt. It worked. Aaron smiled back and moved his chair closer to hers. Now that they were sitting so close together, Addy realized that he smelled nice. She hadn't ever known a boy to have a smell before, but Aaron smelled clean and fresh and just a little bit floral in a complicated, masculine way. Addy wondered if all boys smelled nice when you got close enough. Maybe she would ask Rose if Douglas smelled nice.

The other boys seemed to respect Aaron's proprietary rights, and though she had danced with many of them earlier in the evening, Addy danced only with Aaron for the rest of the night. She felt proud to be singled out by one of the best dancers and better-looking boys in the room and hoped that Harriet noticed.

When the last song was announced, Addy knew she needed to leave quickly if she didn't want to be seen with Rose and Douglas. It wouldn't do to have everybody at the dance realize that she had two people watching her as if she were a child.

"I've quite lost track of time," she said. "My mother's a widow, and I don't want her to worry, so I'll need to be leaving now."

"I had hoped for a long, slow dance with you," Aaron said, as he pulled her to him and moved toward the dance floor.

Addy gently pulled away. "Sorry," she said.

"You're like Cinderella," he said. "You need to leave the ball early."

Addy smiled.

"Can I see you home?" he asked.

"Not tonight. I'm sure we'll meet again. Are you planning to come to other dances?"

"I will now," he said. "Maybe next time you'll drop one slipper, and I'll scour the kingdom looking for you."

Addy laughed, told him goodnight, and walked past Douglas and Rose on her way to get her coat. She was out the door and onto the sidewalk before they caught up with her.

"Are you trying to run out on us?" Rose asked. "If we hadn't been watching, we wouldn't have noticed you leaving."

"I knew you would see me come past your table. I couldn't let that boy think I had two watchdogs following me."

"It looked like you had a good time," Douglas said.

"It looked like you had a good time, too," Addy responded.

"I did."

"Why don't you dance?"

"I'd rather chat. Usually there's no good conversation at these dances, but tonight I brought good conversation with me."

"Flatterer," Rose said and laughed

Addy was not so lost in the wonder of her first dance that she failed to notice something more relaxed and less formal in Rose's relationship with Douglas. When he came back from his trip to the States in the summer, Addy thought that Rose was avoiding him, but now they seemed like old friends. Or maybe this was how brothers treat older sisters, or how plain women respond to the attentions of handsome men. Or perhaps it was the atmosphere of the dance. When she thought about Aaron, she also wondered about the influence of the dance. How would he look in the cold light of day?

Bess was waiting up for them in the living room. She stayed seated in the winged chair sipping her tea as they trooped into the house.

"You're late."

"Actually, we're early. We left just as the last song began," Rose said.

"Did you have a good time? Was it as wonderful as you anticipated, Addy?"

"It was, and more. I danced every dance, and all the boys said I was a terrific dancer. And one boy at the end asked to see me home."

"She's quite right, Mama," Rose said. "Addy was the belle of the ball. And that one young gentleman looked quite smitten."

"Don't you go getting any ideas, Addy. A dance is one thing, but seeing a boy is something else again. I haven't said it's time for that. I don't want any problems from you, young lady."

"He was just a boy who got me a cup of lemonade. And I wasn't the only one who had a good time."

Bess looked at Rose. "Did you have a good time, too?"

"I did," Rose said, looking amused.

"Did you dance?"

"No, I chatted the evening away with Douglas."

Bess looked surprised again. "I assumed you would be dancing, Douglas."

"Not me. I don't like dancing, but I do like chatting."

"Well, thank you for going to the dance. It made me feel much better knowing that somebody was keeping an eye on Addy. Now off to bed with all of you."

As they went upstairs, Addy said, "Thank you, Rose. Because of you, I got to go to the dance and have a good time."

"You're welcome, Addy. I had a good time, too."

"You and Douglas looked quite chummy."

"We're good, old friends, Addy." Rose turned to go into her bedroom and then turned back. "Don't make a mistake and think it more than that. Douglas isn't making that mistake, and I don't want you to, either." Rose went into her room and closed the door behind her.

Addy was taken aback by her sister's vehemence. She hadn't been assuming anything, though she had been surprised to see what a good friend he was.

>———>——>|———————|<——<———<

THE PULL OF HABIT WAS STRONG ENOUGH TO MAKE BREAK-fast the next day seem no different from breakfast on all the days preceding it. As usual, Douglas drank a glass of juice, grabbed a muffin, and rushed out the door, while Rose, Bess, and Addy sat down to porridge and eggs and several cups of tea. After Bess and Rose left for the shop, Addy sat on the back stoop to watch the garden while she relived the excitement of her first dance. As she sat there, a face peeked around the corner of the brick wall, and Addy was startled by the sound of a male voice.

"There you are. I knocked and knocked but there was no answer even though I hadn't seen you leave the house. That's when I decided to check around back."

"Aaron! You were watching the house?" She smoothed her skirt and brushed her hair back from her face before asking, "Why aren't you at school?"

"My first lecture isn't for an hour, and you live close enough for me to make it."

"How did you find out where I live?"

"From the other girls. They weren't shy about telling me."

"That's terrible. A girl can't even trust her friends." Addy shook her head in mock annoyance and smiled. Aaron smiled in return. The sunlight showed the auburn highlights in his hair, and Addy noticed how his eyes widened when he looked at her. She was briefly reminded of the wolf who says, "All the better to see you with, my dear."

"Who were those others who left the house?"

"My mother and my sister and the medical student who boards with us."

"He's a lucky fellow. I'd like to board with you."

"I'm sure my mother won't consider taking another boarder."

"I didn't say I wanted to board with your mother. I said I wanted to board with you," Aaron said and sat on the stoop next to her.

Addy looked at him in dismay. "Don't you be getting fresh. I never heard such talk."

"Don't be mad, Addy. I just wanted to let you know how much I like you. I feel so lucky to have met you that I don't want anybody else to get that lucky besides me."

Now that they were sitting close to one another, Addy could see that he was just as good-looking and his smile was just as charming as it had been at the dance. He still smelled nice, too. Whatever that was, it made him fit right into the garden and set him apart from anybody she'd ever met before. And he felt lucky to have met her. That set him apart, too.

Aaron looked at the garden. "Is this your backyard?"

"Yes. It's my garden, and I think it's my favorite place on earth."

"It's pretty," he said as he stood up.

"Would you like me to show you around?" Addy said, pleased that he had noticed how pretty the garden looked in the morning sun. This will be the second boy I've shown the garden to, she thought, and wondered whether or not to tell Aaron that he wasn't the first.

N.R. King

"A tour of the garden might be fun," he said and set off toward the apple tree.

"Wait. Where are you going? Be careful if you're planning to walk among the flowers."

"Careful of what? Are they dangerous?" Aaron asked. He reached for an apple and stepped on a muscari, crushing it under his foot.

"Now look what you've done. You're the dangerous one." Addy came over to straighten the flower. She frowned as she set it back in the soil. How could anyone be so clumsy and care so little about the damage he caused? Especially someone who wants to be doctor.

"What are you upset about? It's just a flower, and I didn't mean to step on it." With that Aaron picked the apple he had been reaching for and sat in the garden chair to eat it.

"That's my mother's chair. Get up right now."

"She's not here, so why can't I sit in it?"

"My father built it just for her."

"This is a strange family, Addy, but I like you anyway."

"Well, I'm not so sure I like you."

"You don't mean that, Addy. I'm really a nice guy, and I think we should get to know each other better. How about if I come in for a minute? I'd love a cup of tea." Aaron threw his half-eaten apple at the base of the tree and got up.

You're not coming into my kitchen, Addy thought. And if my father was alive or Douglas was home, you'd never suggest such a thing.

"No tea, Aaron. You need to leave," she said.

Aaron followed her up the stoop to the back door, and when she reached for the door knob, he put his hand on her arm. His other arm went around her waist and held her tight as he kissed the back of her neck. Addy was shocked, and she pushed back hard against him. As he tumbled down the three steps, she rushed inside and locked the door.

Aaron brushed himself off and called after her. "You can't blame a fellow for trying. I still get all the Lindy's at the next dance."

Addy crept through the house and peeked out the parlor window. Only when she saw Aaron walking away did she return to the kitchen and sit for a long time at the table. Even though he had frightened her, she was pleased at how well she had handled Aaron's surprise visit. He certainly didn't get his way with me, she thought. I showed him who was boss, and he still wants to see me at the next dance.

Addy vigorously washed the dishes from breakfast and swept the kitchen floor. She took the dust pan outside and was pleased to notice a squirrel making off with Aaron's half-eaten apple. Saves me cleaning it up, she thought, and fattens one of my bushy-tailed friends.

As the more unsettling moments of the visit faded, Addy began to see the romantic aspects. He went to a lot of trouble to find me, she mused, so he can't be all bad. And there's his lovely smile and pretty hair. But she didn't like remembering the shiver she felt when his arm went around her or the feel of his moist lips on the back of her neck. She hoped that didn't count as her first kiss.

Addy decided not to tell Bess about her morning adventure. She didn't tell Harriet, either, even though they spent a whole evening together going over every detail of the dance. Harriet wouldn't say anything on purpose, but she might let something slip, and Addy didn't want to jeopardize her permission to attend dances in the future.

NOBODY BUT ADDY SEEMED TO NOTICE HOW SLOWLY TIME went by until the next dance. For her, ordinary life had become a bore. The only bright spot was the need to create a new outfit. Addy had just three fancy dresses, and she couldn't risk showing up at the next dance in anything that resembled her outfit at the first dance. Her green dress was out because, with its flare skirt and tiny buttons down the back, it was too much like her lavender dress, and she wanted to save her deep rose dress until the winter. Then she found a pattern for a vest in a new knitting magazine. The vest would hide the little buttons, and the fancy yarn and the intricate pattern would transform her green dress into something unique, especially when it was fastened with the pearl brooch Rose had given her for her birthday. I'm about to make this dress even more beautiful than my lavender dress, she thought, and set to work.

Now the days flew by as Addy hurried to finish her new vest with plenty of time to wash and block it before the dance. Fortunately, Aaron did not pay her another surprise visit.

As the date of the second dance approached, Addy reminded her mother that she wanted to go.

"Who else is going?" Bess asked.

"I don't know, but I'll be fine at the dance even if I go by myself."

"You won't be going alone, Addy. Get that idea out of your head right now. I'll see if Rose can go again."

Rose was, indeed, willing to go, and, at breakfast the next morning, Douglas agreed to go again, too. So it was settled, and the three of them set out as before on the night of the dance.

Addy wore her green dress and its fancy vest fastened with her new pearl brooch, and, in the spirit of the occasion,

Douglas wore the tartan scarf Rose had given him years before. Rose accused him of trying to achieve Stewart clan status just by wearing the plaid, even as she acknowledged that the bright red and black colors suited him.

"Who do you hope you'll be mistaken for?" she teased. "A child of Mary, Queen of Scots? Next you'll take to playing the bagpipes and wearing a thistle."

"Or a kilt!" Addy added. "I wonder, Rose, if he's a *sgian dubh* tucked in his sock."

"A dagger in his sock? He'll probably cut his leg."

"Well, he's almost a doctor, so he can stitch himself up again." Addy and Rose and even Douglas had to laugh.

"I never knew a man so beset by his dates to a dance," he said.

"I'm not your date," Addy said, suddenly worried that they meant to keep more of an eye on her than they had last time.

"Don't worry, Addy," Rose said. "We won't get in the way of your good time."

When they arrived at the dance, Addy quickly scanned the room and saw the girls she knew. She didn't see Aaron. "Will you two wait a minute, and let me walk in alone?" she said.

Rose smiled and nodded. "We'll dawdle a minute before we come in. But don't leave the dance without us again."

Addy hurried to join her friends and noticed that Rose and Douglas came in a moment later. They found a table as before, and Douglas got them each a cup of punch. Addy wondered if they would dance and found herself hoping not. There was something ridiculous in seeing a woman as old as Rose laughing with a man as young as Douglas, and it would be even worse to see her dancing with him. Women, especially plain women her age, should be home, not out with men so much younger.

Addy wasn't long with her friends before Aaron rushed up, grabbed her hand, and ran to the dance floor.

"I'm so glad to see you," he said. "I was waiting and waiting. Now the real dancing can begin."

And it did. Addy danced every dance with Aaron, and while she was flattered by his attention, she resented Aaron's assumption that she wanted to dance only with him. She also disliked the way he held her so tightly for the slow dances that she could feel his chest pressing against her breasts. When she looked over at Rose and Douglas, she could see that they didn't like it, either.

After a particularly strenuous Lindy, Aaron parked Addy at a table and told her to wait while he went for lemonade. Addy watched him walk away. There was a spring in his step even when he wasn't dancing, and she thought he looked quite gallant. This boy is not just good-looking, she thought. He's dashing.

As she sat there, a tall, blond boy sat down next to her. "You're some dancer," he said.

"Well, thank you," she answered, lowering her eyes and trying to accept the compliment modestly.

"Maybe we could dance the next one."

"Fine with me," Addy said, and looked up to see Aaron glowering at them. He reminded her of a peacock in full display. Beautiful and fierce all at once.

"Well, it's not fine with me, and you're in my seat," Aaron said.

"Sorry," the blond said, getting up and moving aside.

"And you're talking to my date."

"Sorry, again. I had no idea she was your date. I thought all the girls came in a group."

"Well, you're wrong about this one, so move on."

Addy was amazed and annoyed to see the blond boy walk away and begin a conversation with another girl. Why did he give up so soon? Wasn't she worth a little more fight? Not that she wanted a fight.

"What makes you think I'm your date?" Addy asked, uncertain whether or not to strike an angry pose.

"I thought we had an understanding. I've been to your house, and you said you would dance all the dances with me. I thought that meant you and I were here together."

"Well, you thought wrong," Addy said, angry now in spite of herself. He may be handsome, she thought, but he'll have to work a lot harder than he has so far to get such a promise from me. "You weren't at my house because you were invited, and I don't remember promising you every dance. I don't know why you think you have the right to decide who I will dance with."

"Let's not argue, Addy. We're having too good a time for that." Aaron leaned forward and kissed her cheek. Addy was too stunned to speak. She stared at him in disbelief while he grinned at her. Then she pushed her chair away from the table.

"I'm not having such a good time, anymore. I'm going to dance with that tall, blond boy."

"Not tonight. I have every dance, remember."

"Not anymore," she said. But when she got up to walk away, Aaron grabbed her wrist. Addy didn't know what to do. The last thing she wanted was to make a scene, but she couldn't decide which was worse, being bullied or being humiliated. She was still searching for a response when a deep voice behind her said, "You need to let go of the lady."

"Ah, the boarder," Aaron said, and dropped her wrist.

Then Addy heard Douglas say, "May I have this dance?" Before Aaron could object, she turned around.

"Sure," she said and followed Douglas onto the dance floor.

As the music began, it was immediately clear to Addy why Douglas didn't dance. He couldn't. He simply shuffled to the music without any attention to the fact that dances have steps. At least, she thought, he doesn't draw attention to us.

Aaron watched from the side. At the end of the dance, the blond returned to ask Addy for the next Lindy, and Douglas graciously retired to sit with Rose. Addy smiled at the blond and looked over at Aaron. Would he try to reclaim her, beg her pardon for his highhanded manner, and humbly request another dance? She was disappointed to see him shrug and chose another partner. If that's his attitude, she decided, then, as handsome as he is, it's my attitude, too.

The rest of the evening flew by in a blur of feet and partners, and Addy soon regained her good spirits. Bess waited up for them again, heard what a wonderful evening it had been, and sent everybody to bed. As Addy lay waiting for sleep, she reviewed the reasons why the evening had been such a success. After she had gotten rid of Aaron, all the boys had flocked to dance with her. She never lacked a partner, and more than one had told her how well she danced and a few of them had dared to say that she looked very pretty. Douglas had come to her rescue without embarrassing her, and nobody had related the incident to Bess. A perfect night. She fell asleep thinking that Douglas's curls were too pretty for a man and how glad she was he had grown back his moustache.

The next morning Addy thought the kitchen greeted her with an especially dazzling display of bright sun and dancing motes. It must know that it's my favorite room, she thought, and it wants to celebrate last night, too. She sat at the kitchen table and let her mind wander over the lovely details of the dance.

"Addy, whatever are you doing sitting there like you have nothing better to do?" her mother scolded as she came into the room.

"Sorry. I'll have breakfast started in a jiffy."

"No, you won't. I've a headache this morning, and I've decided to stay home. You'll be at the shop with Rose for the day. Now go upstairs to dress, and I'll get breakfast ready here."

Addy scurried up the stairs, pleased at the sudden change in plans. She enjoyed the hustle and bustle of the shop, and she knew she was good with customers. "You're lovely to take such an interest in my project," they would exclaim as they bought the more expensive ribbon or the shell buttons they now realized were perfect for the sweaters they planned to trim.

"I don't actually mislead them," Addy had once told Rose. "I just help them make a new decision about what they need. I learned how from watching you and Mama, so it's you who should be proud."

"You're a very good student," Rose had responded. "When I watch you with a customer, you remind me of Papa."

Addy had smiled the rest of that day.

THE MORNING PASSED QUICKLY, AND IT WAS NOON BEFORE Addy realized she had forgotten to bring her lunch. Rose sent her home for it. When she came into the house, Addy overheard her mother in the living room saying, "It's the same news this morning as every morning. How am I to take care of them? You have to help me see a way." Addy was surprised that there would be company so early and called out that she had come home to get her lunch. When she went into the parlor, her mother was dusting. Nobody else was there. Bess's look defied her to say that she had overheard anything.

When she got back to the shop, Addy reported the incident to Rose.

"She's talking to Papa," Rose explained.

"Papa?"

"I think she knows better what she's thinking when she says it out loud, and it comforts her to pretend she's saying it to him."

Addy was glad that she had told Rose about overhearing Bess talking to herself, because later in the day, Mrs. Heath came into the shop with the same report.

"It's your mother I've come to speak about," she told Rose while Addy listened from the backroom. "And I'm glad there's no one else here to hear what I've got to say." Mrs. Heath lowered her voice. "She was mumbling to herself in the garden, she was."

Rose's look of concern melted away to her usual look of interest in whatever a customer might have to say. "Thank you for letting me know, Mrs. Heath. Mum had a bit of a headache this morning, and sometimes she hums to herself as it goes away. She says it helps clear the pain, and who of us can say it doesn't."

"I never get headaches, myself," Mrs. Heath said.

"You're a fortunate woman in that," Rose answered. "And we're fortunate girls to have a neighbor so concerned with us and kind enough to come to the shop to let me know about Mum."

Rose's gracious smile and manner protected her from any hint of irony, and Mrs. Heath left the shop gratified by the compliment.

Addy was more concerned than Rose.

"Don't worry, Addy," Rose said, "Mama has had difficult times before. She got through those, and she'll get through this. We just need to be cheerful."

"But outside in the garden?"

Rose laughed. "No ordinary neighbor would have heard her. Just Mrs. Heath."

Bess had finished the housework and fixed dinner by the time Rose and Addy got home, and they all sat down immediately to a hot meal.

"I'm glad you're better, Mama," Addy said. "But you didn't need to do the housework."

"So that's the thanks I get," Bess said.

"I'm not ungrateful, but maybe it would be better to relax instead of doing housework when you have a headache."

"After my headache cleared up, it was nice to be at home. I think I'll stay home for a while now that you're old enough to help in the shop every day, and I'm confident Rose can manage very well without me."

Addy was surprised. Her mother had never been so obvious before in acknowledging that Rose was the one who kept the shop going.

Now Addy and Rose ate and hurried off to the shop, and Bess fixed breakfast, ate with them, and finished dressing later. Douglas still rushed from his room, gulped down tea and toast, grabbed an apple, and left for school while they were still at the table. Bess never failed to tell him that just an apple for lunch was a disgrace, that people would think she didn't know the meaning of "board."

Douglas would laugh and say, "I'll get some real food from students with nice landladies," and hurry out the door. Then Bess would laugh, too, and wish him a good day.

Bess started talking to Joseph as soon as she was alone in the house. The news from Germany dominated her conversation. "Every day there's a new story," she told him, "and every day it's worse than the day before. What am I going to do? Do you remember Mrs. Blum's cousin? The one who lives in Potsdam? Her neighbor said he wasn't Jewish anymore, but a change of heart doesn't matter to the Nazis, and he had to run off to Italy. Where would I run to?" Bess sighed and went upstairs to continue dusting in the bedrooms.

"We always thought that Mrs. Heath was as nosy as they come, and having her right next door peering over her fence to see what we were up to was the only thing wrong with this house. But she's come in handy, at last. Yesterday, she told me she saw a boy go into our backyard not long ago and come out a short time later brushing off the seat of his pants. Seems he must have fallen on his backside, and I've no doubt that our Addy put him there."

Bess sat for a moment on Rose's bed and laughed. "That girl's a spitfire, Joseph. You always loved her spirit. Even when I found her exasperating. She still wears me out."

Bess got to her feet and went back downstairs. She took everything out of the breakfront, dusting each piece and putting it on the dining room table. She lingered over the kiddush cup. "I miss your singing at Shabbos dinner, Joseph, and I know Rose does, too. Sometimes I think I can still hear your voice, and sometimes I'm afraid I can't. Addy probably doesn't remember."

Bess dusted the shelves and set each thing back in its place. "It has to be Addy that gets out, but I'm afraid there isn't enough time to wait for a new medical student to graduate. I hope she meets someone whose mother is as worried as I am and calls her son home early. That way Addy can go with him, and if we all survive, they can come back after Hitler is gone, and the boy can finish medical school." Bess shook her head. "I know that sounds impossible. If only you were here, Joseph, none of this would be happening to us."

Not only was there a hot dinner ready when Addy and Rose came home each evening, there was also likely to be neighborhood news. Other housewives never shared tidbits with Addy, but Bess was on cordial, if distant, terms with her neighbors, and they all enjoyed a cup of tea together in this kitchen or that now and again in the middle of the afternoon. That's how Addy learned that Aaron had found a new girl.

"The Jewish boy from New Jersey that all the mums were looking at, wondering if he would like their daughters, has taken up with Kathleen MacDonald," she announced one evening. "They tell me he showed quite an interest in you, Addy, but now that I see where his eye fell, I'm glad you didn't give him any encouragement. And I'm glad I send you to the dances with your sister to look after you."

Addy was glad that her mother didn't know anything more about her and Aaron, and she wondered how Bess would react if she knew that it was Douglas who had rescued her.

"Our own Douglas doesn't seem to have an eye for the girls, and the mothers have given up on him," Bess continued. "There's talk he has a girl at home." She looked at Rose and Addy for a reaction, but there was none she chose to comment on. "Do you know a boy named Sid, Addy? They say he's a nice boy."

Addy said she hadn't noticed him at any of the dances.

After three weeks at home, Bess surprised Addy again by declaring that she was rested and ready to return to work. Addy asked Rose if she thought Mama was better enough to spend all day at the shop.

"She's fine, Addy. I had forgotten that she did this the year I turned nineteen, too. She's been gathering information about the medical students from the other housewives, and now that she has a good idea of what your prospects are, she probably has a plan in mind."

A plan? She's no right to be making plans and judging prospects, Addy fumed. My prospects will be judged by me, and I won't go about worried that some boy named Sid, who doesn't even go to dances, will show up at dinner one night.

FOR THE NEXT DANCE, ADDY BOUGHT AN INEXPENSIVE PALE pink dress and sewed a new lace collar on it. Its soft look contrasted nicely with what one of her partners at the last dance had called her "saucy manner." Addy had to admit that she loved to flirt, and dancing made little hints of mischief easy. An extra toss of the head or sly smile caught a boy's attention in a gratifying way. She hadn't liked it when Aaron misinterpreted and thought she was being bold, but no other partner had made that mistake since. And as long as she saw these boys only at dances, she was safe.

As usual, Bess had asked Rose to go to the dance as well, and Rose had agreed. On the night of the dance, itself, however, Bess complained of feeling ill.

"You'll have to miss this dance, Addy," Bess said. "I need Rose to stay home tonight."

"I'll be fine by myself. You don't need both of us here, do you?"

"It may be that I do need both of you here, but that's not the point. The point is that you're not going to the dance alone and that's that."

"I won't be alone. The room is full of people, and I'll stay close to Harriet. We'll watch out for each other."

"Harriet? I can't say knowing she'll be there makes me happier to see you go alone."

"Nothing happens at dances but dancing."

"Enough, Addy."

"But it's the safest place in the world. There's no danger at…"

Douglas interrupted. "Do you think Addy will be safe with me there? I had planned to go along with Rose, and I'm still happy to go so that Addy doesn't miss the dance."

Addy smiled at her unexpected ally and took a deep breath. But the confused look on her mother's face checked her impulse to add any further entreaty of her own. She couldn't remember her mother being caught so off guard before.

Bess studied Douglas closely, as if he had become someone she didn't know, before she nodded and answered. "That's very kind of you, Douglas, and a good solution for tonight."

ADDY HOPED THAT NOBODY WOULD THINK DOUGLAS WAS HER date and was relieved when he quickly dispelled any such notion by taking a seat at a table as she went to dance. Although the dancing was as lively as ever and she captured the attention of her usual steady stream of partners, Addy couldn't help noticing Douglas sitting by himself. At one point, she saw a pretty girl wearing too much lipstick and a bright blue dress that didn't suit her sit beside him. He must have discouraged her attention because she got up after only a minute or two.

Douglas sat alone for so long that Addy began to feel sorry for him. He seemed pensive, and she regretted that he was being so poorly paid for accompanying her to the dance.

After she had danced her third Lindy and didn't care about the next foxtrot, Addy sat down at his table. He likes to chat, she thought, and I can be as amusing as Rose.

Douglas smiled as she sat down. "You're a good dancer, Addy, and quite the favorite partner. I hope you're having a good time."

Addy brushed her hair away from her face. "Dancing is fun, but I like chatting, too. And the best dancers aren't the best chatters."

"Are you searching for someone who's both?"

"You can't make a life out of good dancing, so good chatting seems more important."

Douglas nodded. "That's profound, Addy." Douglas was quiet for a minute, and Addy wasn't sure what to say next. What if she wasn't profound again?

"You aren't the little girl I met four years ago," Douglas said.

"That sounds like something my mother would say. Only she'd never admit that I'm not a little girl."

"I'm sure you're right about that."

Douglas laughed, and Addy laughed, too, pleased with herself for having amused him.

She rested her eyes on his face and smiled her best warm, genuine smile. "There's just four years between us. That's nothing, really."

"At this moment, it does seem like nothing," Douglas agreed and then added, "This talk is getting too serious for a dance."

Addy laughed and asked him to get her some punch. While he was away from the table, a boy she had danced with earlier came by and asked her to dance. He wasn't as handsome as some of the boys, but Addy remembered him as a graceful partner. He was a particularly good choice for the next dance, a waltz, because the waltz, though it seems easy, was actually difficult to execute well. She knew they would do it justice.

Addy looked over at Douglas in line to get punch, shook her head and said she was sitting with a friend and needed a rest.

"You? Need a rest? I can't believe that," he said.

"That's what I said, so it must be the truth," she responded and turned away.

When Douglas returned with two cups of punch, she was sitting alone waiting for him. Other boys looked over occasionally, but nobody interrupted them. Addy felt grown up and pleased that others saw a fifth-year student getting her punch and sitting with her. Suddenly Douglas didn't seem like a liability.

After she finished her punch, Addy got up to dance again. As she was truckin' across the floor, wagging her finger and winking at her partner, she noticed Douglas sitting at his table. For a moment he looked like a stranger, and she could understand why that pretty girl had joined him earlier. Douglas was handsome.

He was also charming and kind and strong and smart and helpful. A man who cared about her and kept her safe. A man she could trust.

The music changed, and Addy felt herself whisked off for a waltz. Her partner skillfully moved them around the other couples, whirling and spinning in perfect time to the music. How lovely to have a dance partner who looks good truckin' and also understands the waltz.

Addy knew she had to focus on her partner if she didn't want to get dizzy. She had fallen down enough times in Harriet's living room to appreciate the danger. The challenge was one of the exciting things about the waltz, and she tried to focus on the steps. But her eyes lingered on Douglas every time she came near his table. She saw that he was smiling at her and felt a rush of feelings that confused her and brought tears to her eyes.

Douglas was still smiling when she whirled past him again. She was moving so fast in ever widening circles that concentration was necessary or she might stumble. Despite the danger, Addy's found herself wondering if Douglas was as content as he pretended to be. Maybe he smiled to hide the awkwardness he felt sitting alone on the sideline all evening. She knew he didn't want to dance, but maybe he wanted to go home.

When the music finally ended, she thanked her partner, politely refused his offer of a cup of punch, and approached Douglas's table.

"Do you want to go home?" she asked.

"I can't leave you here. Your mother would kill me." They both laughed.

"She would, indeed. But the dance is nearly over."

"Are you sure? We won't leave before you are ready."

"If we leave now, we'll have an easier time finding our coats, so let's go." She didn't add that she would rather walk home with him than dance again, or how surprising she found that realization.

Addy felt so happy walking beside Douglas on the way home, that she took his arm and matched her step to his. Douglas put his hand softly over hers and hummed a tune from the dance. When she recognized it, Addy hummed along with him.

As if lost in thought, Douglas began to sing the words. "I love you, yes I do, I love you. If you break my heart, I'll die."

Addy looked over at him and noticed that he was looking resolutely ahead. Of all the songs he could have chosen, why did he pick that one? Does he also feel a difference in our relationship? She joined him in singing the next lines. "So be sure it's true when you say I love you. It's a sin to tell a lie."

"I didn't know you paid so much attention to the music at dances, Douglas," Addy said. When he didn't answer, they walked in silence for a long time, and Addy found herself thinking that Prince Charming might not be tall, might speak with a little stammer, might not know how to dance. His cruel father, the king, probably forced him to give the ball in the story even though he knew his son would sit at a table the whole night, and it would be up to the most beautiful maiden in the realm to sit next to him in order to catch his fancy.

Matching his stride to hers when they crossed the street, Douglas moved her to walk next to the buildings and took her other arm in his. There's something in that gesture, Addy thought. He does understand. The idea excited her. That he's almost finished his schooling means less time to wait before we can marry and sail away and live happily ever after. Mother will be upset, of course. If she intended Douglas to marry either of us, it must be Rose she had in mind. But that plan doesn't seem to have worked. Still, Addy knew her mother would be furious, so it was essential that Bess didn't catch on until it was too late and there was nothing she could do about it. I can do this, Addy thought. I just need to make him forget about that girl they say he has in the States.

As they came up the walk to the house, Addy could see her mother knitting in the parlor. Douglas hesitated at the front door, and then gently took her arm from his before he reached for the knob and opened the door so she could go in first.

The Girl in the States

1937

ADDY WOKE EARLY THE MORNING AFTER THE DANCE AND began her campaign to win Douglas. She took a scoop of salad cream from the Heinz jar, crumbled in some tarragon and added a bit of mustard and a dash of onion salt. He hasn't ever had anything like this, she thought, as she spread the mixture on bread and arranged several chicken slices and crisp lettuce leaves on top before gently cutting the sandwich in half along the diagonal and wrapping it. Carrot and celery sticks in wax paper, a teabag, and napkins also went into the sack. When she heard Douglas in the bathroom, Addy snuck into his room and put the lunch in his satchel before Rose and Bess came downstairs. He rushed through the kitchen some time later, drank his tea, grabbed an apple and a piece of toast, and left the house as usual. Addy wondered what he would think at lunchtime. Would he taste the tarragon?

When Addy came into the kitchen the next morning, she found two perfect, pink carnations pinned to the paper bag she had used for his lunch and propped up on the sink where she would see them before Rose and Bess appeared for breakfast. She sniffed the blossoms and then took a deep breath of the fresh, spicy scent. Real flowers. He's brought real flowers, at last. After fixing his lunch, Addy set it just inside Douglas's bedroom door. No need to hide it in the satchel. He would know it was for him and that it was from her.

Each day, the paper bag came back with a lovely, little gift attached. Sometimes a flower, sometimes a piece of fruit, sometimes a pretty button, sometimes a tin of candies.

Addy was relieved that Douglas never betrayed any change in his manner toward her, and it added to her delight that Bess was oblivious to what was going on under her very nose. But what was going on? Addy supposed that the little gifts could be a sign of brotherly affection, but their walk home from the dance and their secrecy now promised something else. She had started it, but he had understood it, and Addy believed she was being wooed in a delicious, secret, wordless way.

On a Tuesday afternoon some weeks later, Bess said she was too tired to stay at the shop until closing. "But, as weary as I am, I still want to get a few things on the way home. Rose, you'll come shopping with me, and Addy, you'll close up tonight. Be sure to leave on time and come right home."

Rose seemed surprised. "Did you say that you would like me to shop with you and Addy to close up?"

"That's right. Let's hurry along so we don't find a crowd at the store."

Addy was pleased that Bess entrusted her with closing the shop for the night. There were no more customers, and at 5:00, Addy turned the sign in the window to indicate that the shop was closed, locked the door, and went to the back room to get her coat and hat. An unopened box of grosgrain ribbon sat on the table, and Addy decided to unpack it and check the contents against the packing slip as she had seen Rose do many times before. Then she planned to put the ribbon on the shelf and the packing slip on Rose's desk to surprise her in the morning. As she worked, she heard a key turn in the lock of the shop door. It must be Annie to clean, or maybe Rose came back. Addy hurried to the front of the shop to see who was there. It was Douglas with his back to her as he relocked the door and put his key in his coat pocket.

"What are you doing here?" she said. Douglas jumped at the sound of her voice, and Addy laughed.

"Addy? You startled me. I thought everybody would have gone home by now."

"Why are you here? I thought Annie cleaned for us because you're so busy, and if you are cleaning, why are you so early?"

"Your mother gave Annie the month off, and I have my old job back for a while. My schedule at the hospital varies a lot, and I fit in the cleaning whenever I can."

"You should tell Mother when they change your schedule."

"I did tell her."

Addy was surprised and at a loss for an explanation.

"She must have forgotten," she said at last, and busied herself with organizing the bins of buttons and wondering if their courtship was about to become more serious. It was one thing to dream of sailing across the ocean with Douglas, and quite another to find herself alone in the empty shop with him. She was both relieved and disappointed when he took off his coat and went immediately to the back room for his rags and mops and bucket of water.

"You can leave now," he called to her, "and when you get home, you can remind your mother that I came to clean."

Addy was still reorganizing the buttons when Douglas reappeared and began to dust the shelves behind the counter, straightening the merchandise as he worked. Addy felt awkward in a pleasantly exciting way.

"Thanks for all the presents," she said. "I love them."

"You're welcome. Thanks for my lunch. It's always delicious. And thanks for the tea." Douglas stopped refolding a stack of scarves and turned to face her. "You're very thoughtful."

"Thanks. You're pretty thoughtful, yourself."

Addy continued to sort the buttons until Douglas finished the mopping. When she looked up, he was moving toward the back room, struggling to carry all the rags and manage the mop and bucket at the same time. He was hunched over and looked just about to fall. Addy laughed.

"You look like a juggler who's lost control of all the things he's trying to keep in the air."

Just as Addy bent to take the rags from him, Douglas lost his balance, dropped everything and fell to the floor, pulling her after him. Laughing, she landed on his lap, and before her laugh could fade, he kissed her.

Is it possible, Addy thought, to be surprised and not surprised at the same time?

"You're beautiful, Addy, and delicious too," Douglas said and kissed her again. This time she found herself responding. His lips were soft, and his moustache was prickly in an unsettling, masculine way. Addy moved so that he could reach her better, and as his arms went around her, his hand touched her breast just lightly. It didn't occur to Addy to protest.

Douglas held her and Addy rested against him for quite a while before she said, "We're lucky the bucket didn't spill."

"We are, indeed," he said and he kissed her again.

"We can't sit on the floor of the shop forever, Douglas. Now that it's a good while past closing time, Mother will be looking for me."

After Addy helped him take the cleaning materials to the back closet, Douglas put on his coat and stood at the door

N.R. King

of the shop for a long moment. Finally, he turned to her and said, "I've wanted to kiss you for a long time, Addy. I hope it's what you wanted, too." And he left.

Addy straightened her blouse and used the mirror in the back room to fix her hair. She thought she looked a little flushed.

"Well, who wouldn't be flushed after her first kiss," she told her reflection. "And her second and her third." She smoothed her hair and pulled her hat on. It seems I've actually decided it's to be Douglas who takes me away as the wife of a doctor.

Addy put on her coat, left the shop, and was nearly home before she remembered the box of grosgrain ribbon. When she got home, she didn't mention Douglas, but she did tell Rose that she had started to check the ribbon for her but had noticed how late it was and hadn't stayed to finish the job.

"That was a good decision," her mother said and then told stories of her little spending spree with Rose.

Not the only good decision I've made lately, Addy thought. You might be surprised to learn how little you know.

It seemed to Addy that Douglas had begun to forget his lunch with increasing frequency, forcing him to return to the house after Bess and Rose had left for the shop. She also realized that she had begun to expect him and no longer tied an old scarf around her head when she dusted or wore the apron she used to wear when she cleaned the bathrooms.

When Douglas came back, they sat together on the stoop or at the kitchen table if the weather was nasty while he told her more about his family. Addy heard about his wonderful mother, his tall, handsome brother who showed signs of becoming a ne'er-do-well, his silly, well-meaning brother, and his sweet little sister. But whenever Addy asked about his father, Douglas said, "The less said about him, the better," and changed the subject.

They also kissed, and more. Addy was shocked by what she thought of as his lust, and even more shocked by her own. But she wouldn't take off her blouse and when he suggested that they lie down together on his bed, or on hers, she became frightened and cried. Then Douglas hugged her and apologized.

One chilly day, they decided to sit outside on the back stoop in spite of the weather. The sun was bright, but the garden was in its wintery mode. The new growth had yet to show, and the apple blossoms were still weeks away. They sat quietly side-by-side, each cradling a cup of hot tea and blowing on the steaming liquid. Addy loved these silent times sitting near Douglas. It made them seem established.

"It was hard growing up with a father like mine," Douglas suddenly said. "My father never worked a day in his life, but he's always well dressed, strutting around town like he's the mayor while the rest of the family wears mended hand-me-downs from our cousins. I grew up hating him and swearing I'd never be like him."

Addy took a tiny sip of tea and wondered what brought on this revelation about his father.

"How does your family manage?" she asked.

"My mother cooks for a little delicatessen. All day and night there are pots of meat boiling on the stove and pans of chickens roasting in the oven. In the morning, she packages it all up and goes to the deli to make sandwiches to sell for lunch. There's also rent money from the upstairs tenants." Douglas sipped his tea. "When her father died, my mother inherited some money, and she bought a two-family house. I begged her not to put the house in Dad's name, and she listened to me. At least he can't lose this house in a poker game. That happened once, and my mother had to take all four of us to cry in front of the man who had won it."

"That's terrible, Douglas. I'm sure you'll never be the kind of man who doesn't support his family."

"It's worse than that, Addy." Douglas looked down. "My father has girlfriends. Do you know what I mean?"

Addy was shocked. But she managed to reply in an even tone, "I do."

"That's the reason I hate him. I hate him for humiliating my mother. She's a beautiful woman who never did anything to deserve this. I'll never forgive him."

"And you shouldn't. That's unforgivable behavior."

"When I get married, it will be to somebody I know I can love and respect forever. Once I'm married, there'll be no fooling around for me. You must know there are girls who like to carry on with lots of medical students. And some medical students carry on with lots of girls. Nobody wants to marry people like that. Marriage is forever, with no fooling around."

Addy didn't say anything. Her friend Holly's father had a girlfriend, but he was the exception. She knew of no other instances and had always assumed that her own husband would never think of other women. She was pleased that Douglas was firm about his commitment to his future wife, but she wondered why he needed to be so adamant.

"I know you won't be like your father. You're nothing like him now, so why would you be like him after you're married?"

Douglas put his teacup on the stoop and tilted her face toward him. He kissed her, stroked her hair, and kissed her again. "I'm falling for you, Addy Kaminsky," he said.

Addy flushed with pleasure but didn't say anything in return. So much for the girl in the States, she thought. If

I ever meet her, I'll be sure she knows who won Douglas's heart. She may have had his attention first, but I'll show her that she didn't stand a chance after he met me.

><>>|————|<<—<

ADDY COULDN'T QUITE BELIEVE THAT BESS WAS OBLIVIOUS TO the romance flourishing in her own house and finally decided that Bess still saw her as a child, not as a woman who might interest somebody like Douglas. That her mother's attitude was both a tribute to Douglas and an insult to her seemed typical, and Addy laughed to think that, in this case, it shielded her from scrutiny. If her relationship with Douglas had escaped Bess's notice, Addy soon realized that it hadn't escaped Rose's.

One morning, Rose forgot her shawl and returned home to find Addy and Douglas having tea in the kitchen. Addy was relieved that Rose hadn't come home a few minutes earlier. It was embarrassing enough when she did come through the kitchen door.

"Rose, what a surprise," Addy said. "Douglas has only just come back, himself, to get a book he forgot and then he was so cold, I made him a cup of tea."

"Oh, Addy, hush. You don't have to explain anything to me. I'm not blind." She patted Addy's arm. "If I had known you had company this morning, I would have made more noise at the front door," she teased.

Addy blushed and looked away.

"Douglas," Rose added in a serious tone, "I assume your intentions are honorable."

"I'm just having tea with your sister. Don't go jumping to conclusions. And no need to alarm your mother."

Rose looked at him sharply before retrieving her shawl from her room and leaving for the shop.

"Do you think she'll tell Mother?" Addy asked.

"No, I don't."

The evidence indicated that he was right. Bess and Rose had plans to see a movie on the night of the next dance, and Bess asked Douglas to keep an eye on Addy.

"I hope you aren't busy and that you don't mind," Bess said, and smiled when Douglas answered, "I'm happy to watch over Addy at the dance. Don't worry about her at all."

Addy was amazed at Bess's complacency as she and Douglas left the house together. The evening started with the usual round of dances and the usual array of partners, but Addy's heart wasn't in it. At the next break in the music, she approached Douglas's table and suggested that they take a walk. Before she knew it, they had walked nearly all the way home.

"Are you sorry you didn't stay at the dance, Addy?"

"No. It seems I would rather walk with you than dance with other boys," she said.

I'm content with him, she thought, and he knows it and feels the same way. Imagine me preferring a man who can't dance. Preferring him to every boy I've ever met.

Addy took Douglas's arm and walked close to him. "Did you ever have a girlfriend, Douglas?"

"I did have one girlfriend, but it didn't work out, and it was a long time ago."

"Was she pretty?"

"No, I don't suppose most people would call her pretty."

"Could she cook?"

"She could make simple things to eat."

Addy was pleased that this old girlfriend didn't sound like much of a rival.

"Where does she live?"

"That's not important, Addy."

"Do you still think about her?"

"I won't pretend that I don't, but only to wish her happiness, and I know that's what she wishes me."

They walked quietly together for several blocks before Addy asked, "What was her name?"

"That doesn't matter. I don't want her for my wife, and that's all that's important now."

Not quite all that's important, Addy thought. There's more to be said.

"Do you have a girlfriend now?" she asked.

Douglas brought her hand to his lips and kissed her fingertips. "What do you think?" he said.

Addy recognized the seriousness of their mood and pressed herself against his side. Why doesn't he say more? I'm sure I love him, and I need to hear him say he loves me, too, and wants to marry me. Think of it. The wife of a senior medical student. Won't Harriet take notice!

When they got home, Addy brought out the rest of the pie from dinner and put the kettle on to boil. They ate and chatted, and then Douglas helped her wash and dry the dishes, with time out for kissing now and again. Addy knew Rose and Bess could be expected any time, but she hoped that they would be delayed a bit longer. Now that her goal was clear to her, Addy was impatient to hear exactly what Douglas had in mind.

"You looked uncomfortable when Rose asked you about your intentions. Do you have intentions, Douglas?"

If Douglas was surprised by such a direct question, he didn't show it. "I do."

Addy waited for him to say more before she continued, "Are they honorable?"

N.R. King

"They are."

Addy waited again before she asked, "Is it time to speak of them?"

"It is."

Now Addy thought she was being teased and became annoyed.

Finally, Douglas said, "Aren't you going to ask what they are?"

"No, I'm not. If there's any asking to be done, you'll have to be the one doing it."

Before he could respond, they heard the front door open and Rose's voice call out a greeting from the foyer.

"Why aren't you two at the dance?" Bess said as she came into the kitchen.

"We were at the dance, and I had a very good time," Addy said. "But I got tired, and we came home. Come have some pie."

Addy bustled about the kitchen putting out plates and cups for them and hoping Bess wouldn't notice her slightly disheveled appearance, or if she did, would think it was the result of dancing. She needn't have worried. Bess's only interest was in talking about the movie she and Rose had just seen.

THE NEXT DAY, THE ONE SUNDAY OF THE MONTH WHEN HE did not need to report to the hospital, Douglas lingered in the parlor after lunch. Bess had gone upstairs for a nap, and Rose was having lunch with two of her friends. That left Addy and Douglas alone downstairs, and Addy with the realization that her mother had not permitted such a thing before. She must have assumed he would be leaving for the hospital, Addy thought, and she must have forgotten that Rose isn't home.

Even though they had the parlor to themselves, Douglas wanted to go out. Addy put on her coat and hat and met him at the front door. He looked charming wearing the new cap she had given him for Chanukah.

"Where shall we go?" Addy asked.

"Let's go to The Meadows. It's my favorite park."

They walked for a time talking about the weather until Addy finally said, "You seem a good deal more interested in the weather than usual, Douglas. Could it be there's something you're trying not to talk of?"

Douglas smiled at her. "You're a perceptive woman, Addy. There is something on my mind."

When he didn't continue, Addy also got quiet. *If he's going to talk, I'll have to let him get to it in his own time. I don't mind waiting, but I'm not talking about the weather anymore.*

When they arrived at The Meadows, Douglas chose a quiet spot on the grass far from the men playing soccer and the children playing tag. Addy wrapped her coat around herself and sat down. Douglas sat facing her. He took some time getting comfortable.

"Addy, you know I'm going home in a few months."

Addy nodded. *Here it comes,* she thought. *Either he'll take me with him, or he's about to make his exit.*

"We've gotten to know each other in a new way in the past months, and I think you will agree that we get on together very well."

Addy nodded again.

"We've never said how we feel about each other, and that's my fault. Whenever I wanted to say something, I couldn't find exactly the right time or exactly the right words. I couldn't expect you to speak first, but I think you feel the same way about me as I feel about you."

Addy stayed quiet and wondered if she was ready to hear what he might say next.

"You know my family is different from yours. There's lots more of them for one thing, and they are lots louder and ruder for another. But I know they will love you as much as I do." Douglas took two deep breaths and then, in a rush, said, "So, will you come home with me?"

Addy looked at him. This was a roundabout way to put things.

"Oh, Addy, don't look at me like that. I see that I'm making a mess of the most important moment of my life. I know I'm asking a lot. You're still young, and I'm asking you to give up everything and follow me to a place you've never seen. Maybe it's too unfair."

Addy reached across the space between them and took his hand. "What exactly are you asking, Douglas?"

"You know."

Addy smiled at him. "I think I do, but I insist on hearing the very words."

Douglas laughed. "Okay, let me see if I can do this right."

Douglas helped her to her feet and knelt on one knee before her. He took both her hands in his and looked into her eyes. "Addy Kaminsky, I love you, and I want you to be my wife and come with me to live in the States when I graduate. Will you marry me?"

Addy laughed and pulled him to his feet. "Oh, Douglas, you sweet, romantic man. I love you, too, with all my heart, and, yes, I'll marry you and go with you wherever you go."

Douglas hugged her, and right there in the park, he kissed her, and she didn't mind at all. Even when a cheer went up from a group of women sitting on a nearby park bench.

"You've got yourself a lovely lass," one of them called out. "Mind that you take good care of her."

"I know I'm a lucky man," Douglas answered. "And I plan to make her happy."

When they were again sitting comfortably on the grass, Douglas reached into his coat pocket. "I brought this along in case you said yes right away," he said and handed her a small box. Coiled inside was a single strand of pearls. Addy held up her hair so he could fasten the clasp for her.

"They're beautiful, Douglas. I've never had anything so lovely."

"My mother sent them from home last month. They were a gift from my father when they became engaged, and she always said I could have them for my bride."

Addy liked the sound of that. She was about to be somebody's bride.

"I didn't want to take anything my father bought, but my mother said that he had no money when they became engaged, and my grandmother bought the pearls so my mother would not be shamed by having no engagement gift. I don't want you to be shamed, either." Douglas sat back for a moment and looked at her. "You look very beautiful wearing them, but you must take them off before we get home and keep them in the box until I have a chance to speak to your mother."

Addy nodded her assent, but immediately added, "Don't take too long. I want everybody to know I'm engaged."

"I need to choose the right moment, but I'll make it soon. Remember, don't tell a soul."

THAT NIGHT, BEFORE GOING TO BED, ADDY TOOK OUT HER pearls and admired them. Now I know I'm somebody's favorite person, she thought. And now I have two favorite people because, though I love Douglas and I'll be going home with him, he doesn't push Rose out of my heart, even if he does come a little ahead of her.

Addy tucked the pearls back in the box. I can't wait to show them to Harriet and tell her about the proposal in the park and the old ladies who cheered. I'll tell her it was all I could do not to cheer right along with them. Maybe she'll cheer, too.

Maybe she'll say, "Addy, you lucky girl! How clever of you to have chosen a senior, and how wonderful that he loves you so much that he gave you his mother's beautiful pearls."

Harriet's too good a friend to say "He's so old." or "He can't dance." Holly might say that, but not Harriet. She'll see how perfect Douglas is.

And she'll probably say, "I'll be lonely without you." I'll have to reassure her that her Prince Charming will show up any minute, and though he might not be a senior or as wonderful as Douglas, he will love her with his whole heart, and maybe I'll see her in the States one day.

THE NEXT MORNING AT BREAKFAST, NOBODY NOTICED ADDY'S change in status. That was hard to believe. With a strange sense of unreality, she watched Douglas hide his lunch in his satchel, gulp down his tea, grab a piece of toast and an apple, and rush out. She watched Rose and Bess leave for the shop, and she watched herself gather the dust cloths and the mop she needed to clean the upstairs bedrooms. She was cleaning in her mother's room when Douglas let himself in the back door and came upstairs. The sound of footsteps frightened Addy, and she shrieked when he came into her mother's room.

"Oh, Douglas. You gave me a fright. Don't ever do that again."

"Sorry, Addy. I came back to have a minute with my wife," he said and took her in his arms.

When his kisses became urgent, Addy grew frightened and stepped away from him.

"Stop, Douglas. We've been good so far, and we'll have to be better now. I love you, and I don't want to fight you off or think I'm disappointing you. I need to feel safe with you."

"You don't have to be afraid of me, Addy. I'll never hurt you." He held her gently, and sprinkled her face with little kisses that made her laugh.

"I've as much fear of myself as I have of you," Addy said. "Talk to my mother soon, and then we'll plan our wedding. I promise you it won't be a long engagement."

>>>>>·———·<<<<

DOUGLAS DID NOT SPEAK TO BESS THAT DAY OR THE DAY after, and Addy became more and more impatient. When Harriet dropped by to talk about the next dance, it was difficult for Addy to feign interest in such childish concerns.

"You seem distracted," Harriet said. "What's wrong?"

Addy almost told Harriet everything right then and there, but she somehow managed to reply, "I haven't anything new to wear, and I'm thinking about how to dress up one of my old outfits."

She was relieved when Harriet left, apparently satisfied with their conversation.

Two days later, Douglas had yet to speak to Bess, and Addy was beside herself. A secret engagement was worse than no engagement at all. Why did he delay? After dinner she knocked softly on Douglas's door.

"Rose is out again tonight," Addy whispered. "And Mama is by herself in the parlor right now. What are you waiting for?"

"I need the right moment," Douglas answered. "Be patient just a little longer."

Addy was lying awake in bed when she heard Rose come home and then the whistle of the kettle boiling on the stove. Rose must be having tea, she thought, and got out of bed. Putting on her robe, and listening for a moment to be sure there was no sound from her mother's room, Addy slipped the pearls into her pocket. I'll just tell Rose, she thought. She should be the first to know anyway. I've only one sister, and I can't be expected to go on keeping a secret from her.

She hesitated a moment in the doorway and turned back to tuck *Howards End* in her other pocket. I'll tell Rose it was my favorite birthday gift because, just like the two of us, nothing could come between the sisters in the book. Armed with a reason for being out of bed if her mother suddenly appeared or if she decided not to show Rose the pearls, Addy crept down the stairs, and peered around the corner. The dining room table was like a long finger pointing toward the kitchen, and the tall breakfront loomed along the wall, expressionless except for one sparkling point where her father's silver kiddush cup caught a bit of the light from the kitchen's overhead fixture.

The kitchen seemed unnaturally bright. Addy noticed the dishtowel, still neatly folded where she had placed it after dinner. But the cupboard stood open, wantonly displaying its stacks of dishes and cups hanging by their handles on hooks along the top of the shelf. Surprisingly, the breakfast things she had set out had been pushed aside, and two old, chipped cups without saucers had been placed on the table. Even more astonishing, Addy saw Douglas sitting at the table with Rose.

Something about the scene made Addy feel like an intruder and stopped her from joining them. Perhaps it was her sense that she was the audience, standing in the dark, watching a performance on a well-lit stage that seemed miles away. Or maybe it was their easy domesticity, the impression that they had done this many times before.

After her initial shock, Addy felt an inexplicable dread. What could this mean? She came a few steps closer and heard Douglas thank Rose for the tea. Addy was surprised that Rose knew how he liked it.

"I've been waiting to talk to you," Douglas said.

"So that's why you scared me half to death sitting in the dark in the parlor."

"I'm sorry I frightened you, but you're a hard woman to catch."

"Don't start, Douglas. You appear to have recovered." There was a long silence and when she spoke again, Rose's voice was soft and her tone was gentle. "I'm sorry, Douglas. I shouldn't tease you. You always knew I wouldn't leave my mother or the shop, and you must believe me when I say my decision makes me happy."

"I do believe you."

"Now believe that I also want you to be happy."

"I am happy, and I plan to make Addy happy, too. We're engaged and plan to be married before I graduate."

Rose sat back in her chair and smiled. "That's wonderful news, Douglas. I'm so pleased for you and Addy."

"You're the first to know, Rose."

"Thank you. Now drink your tea."

Douglas sipped his tea and then spoke so softly that Addy had to strain to hear him. "I don't know that I'll ever have a better friend than you."

"You'll certainly have a better wife," Rose said, and laughed.

She leaned toward Douglas and continued their quiet conversation. But their words could no longer be heard.

Addy crept back up the stairs and crawled under the covers wishing she had never gotten out of bed. Now she understood Douglas's delay in seeing her mother and why he had made her promise to keep their engagement a secret. It was Rose's blessing he needed, and it made him happy and sad at the same time to ask for it. Rose was the girl in the States.

Addy stared at the ceiling, and willed away her tears. Even though a romantic relationship between Rose and Douglas was impossible to imagine, Addy found herself imagining it. Had they kissed? What if they had done more than that? Well, what if they had? What do I have to cry about? I can have any boy I want. They'll line up for me just like they line up to dance with me. They'll fall at my feet and beg me to marry them, and then I'll go across the ocean with a boy who never loved anyone else.

I'm glad to know that Douglas betrayed me with my own sister, and I won't be the consolation prize. I'm no one's second choice. He can go home alone. I'll send him packing just like Rose did.

Addy turned over and closed her eyes. Of course, I'll have to give back the pearls. And one day some other girl will get them. And Douglas will fasten them around her neck and tell her how beautiful she looks wearing them. And I'll go on living here and working in the shop. Dusting in the morning and selling buttons in the afternoon. What if I go to dances for years until I'm the oldest girl in the room and there is no other beau? What if I grow old being nagged by Mama all day, and sitting around the radio every evening worrying about the Nazis and reading letters from Harriet and Holly about life in the States?

Addy sat up in bed. The idea that Douglas actually fell for Rose, plain, old, unromantic Rose, suddenly struck her as absurd. He probably loved me from the moment he saw me. But I was just a child, and he had to wait for me to grow up before he could court me. Rose never meant a thing to him. It was never her. I was the reason no other girl ever caught his eye. It was always me. I was the girl in the States.

Addy shook out her pillow and settled herself under the covers. It's not his fault that Rose told herself fanciful stories. It's Mama's fault for meddling and pushing Rose at him and Rose's fault for not seeing that he was just being polite. It's all a figment of her imagination, and Douglas is too kind to set her straight. Poor thing. She's about to be left alone with Mama and a lifetime of working in the shop. So she clings to the notion that Douglas loved her and she's the one who gave him up. What could be more absurd than that?

I've no use for a sister who thinks my husband fancied her first, who thinks she's putting one over on me. I've no use for such a sister at all. I'm the one he wants to marry and take far, far away from here. I'll be a doctor's wife in a big house with beautiful things and a handsome husband who adores me and lovely children, and friends who envy me. All the things Rose will never have.

Addy knew that if she never spoke of what she had just seen, it could not become part of her story. She could make it disappear. Along with Rose and her mother and the whole of Edinburgh.

ADDY CAME INTO THE KITCHEN THE NEXT MORNING TO SEE the cupboard closed and the breakfast things carefully returned to their usual places on the table. There was no evidence of the two old cups. But this was no longer Addy's favorite room. This was a kitchen with secrets, with other loyalties. Even the sun streaming in from the garden could not cleanse it of shadows. This room could not be trusted.

Rose came down to breakfast as sunny as the kitchen, itself, and showered Addy with good cheer. "It's a grand morning, Addy," she said and took the wooden spoon from Addy's hand. "Let me stir that for you on this bright, beautiful day."

Addy relinquished the spoon and stepped away from the stove. On any other day she would have been caught up in the banter and answered with smiles and quips of her own. But now she steeled herself against the onslaught by remembering that if Rose was as sunny as the kitchen, she was also as duplicitous. A few smiles can't fool me, she thought. I see right through you. You're no sister to me.

"We've yet to talk about *Howards End*, Addy. What did you think of Margaret and Helen?"

"I thought they were ridiculous. Margaret would never have sided with Helen against her husband's wishes. Any woman would choose her husband over her sister. The stupid ending ruined the whole book."

Rose looked confused for a moment but didn't pursue the discussion. Just as well, Addy thought, or she might have caught an even bigger earful.

That evening, Douglas came into the kitchen as the three women finished dinner and asked to speak with Bess in the parlor. Rose looked at Addy, but Addy quickly busied herself clearing the table. She didn't want Rose to be any part of this.

After a few minutes, Bess and Douglas emerged, and Bess took the good Scotch and four glasses from the dining room breakfront. It was an old bottle that Joseph had bought many years before.

"It's a wonderful night for a *l'chaim* with your father's Scotch," she said. Douglas grinned while Bess poured a generous amount in each glass. Addy kept her eyes on her mother as they all raised their glasses and Bess said, "Tonight we celebrate the engagement of Dovid ben Moshe to Aidel bas Yosef. May their union be blessed with happiness. *L'chiam, l'chaim.*" Everybody drank, and the ladies coughed and choked a little, and their eyes ran with tears from the emotion of the moment or from the liquor. Then everybody laughed and talked at once.

When Bess hugged her, Addy realized that she couldn't remember the last time her mother had touched her. "It's a brave thing you are doing, Addy," her mother said. "Your father will be so proud and pleased knowing you'll be safe." References to her father as if he were still alive confused Addy enough that she didn't wonder until later why her mother called her brave for marrying Douglas.

Rose also rushed to hug her and said, "I couldn't be happier for you, Addy. I'll miss having you here, but I'll know that you are where you want to be."

"Thank you, Rose," Addy said and stepped back. She wondered at her sister's hypocrisy. Rose seemed genuinely pleased that it was Addy who would marry Douglas and travel to America.

When Rose hugged Douglas, their cheeks brushed, and Addy knew that she could never trust Rose again. She knows that Douglas is too kind to pull back from her embrace, Addy thought. The sooner I get him away from Edinburgh, the better.

The very next day, Bess went to see the rabbi who put them on the calendar in just a bit over two months. The preparations for the wedding began in the midst of preparing the house for Passover and putting the spring items on display in the shop.

Now that Addy and Douglas were engaged, Bess never left them alone in the house. She stayed home in the mornings to cook, while Addy and Rose went to the shop. The hired girl cleaned the shop, and Douglas was told to concentrate on completing his graduation requirements. Bess even slept with her door open. But she needn't have worried. Addy didn't want to be with Douglas. She wanted to be carried along by the rush of events until there was no time to think or inclination to look back. She only wanted to look ahead and put her mother's house and everybody in it far behind her.

Rose helped find the perfect dress and added lace from Belgium and tiny seed pearls she had been saving for a special occasion, carefully concealing each tiny stitch so the trim seemed to flow out of the fabric itself. The guest list was checked and rechecked. There were Addy's friends, and Douglas's friends from school and some of his professors, and there were Rose's friends and Bess's friends and those friends who remembered Joseph and had been kind to the family when he died. The only people coming from the States were Clara and Max, Douglas's parents, though Douglas assured Addy that there were relatives galore waiting to meet her when they got home.

Bess insisted that Joseph's name be added to the guest list, and that Addy and Douglas go to the cemetery to invite him to the wedding. Addy knew about this custom because her friend Eileen had gone to the cemetery to invite her grandfather to her wedding the previous winter. Poor Eileen had given in to Mr. Blum's nephew, and now she was married to a butcher's assistant and living two doors down from her parents. Berel was a happy-go-lucky boy always ready with a smile and a joke, but Addy still wondered why Eileen had given up so easily.

Douglas was horrified by the idea of taking an invitation to the cemetery. "I thought we were going to put all these old superstitions behind us," he complained.

Addy knew Douglas's views on religion, and they didn't worry her. She would be doing the cooking after they were married, so it would be easy to avoid the foods she couldn't imagine eating. Beyond that, she didn't care. It might be sad to give up Friday night dinners, but Addy knew Douglas would not find the joy in them that her father had.

"We will when we have our own home," she said. "But we don't want to start a row with Mother. It isn't worth it. It's a lovely long walk to the cemetery, just a minute or two there, and then a lovely walk back. We'll take a picnic lunch and eat at the park on our way home."

Douglas was mollified, and the next Sunday they set out with a picnic basket and an invitation to leave on the grave.

When they got to Joseph's grave, Addy said, "You would have liked my father, Douglas. He was the nicest man I ever knew." And then added, "Before I met you, of course." She put the invitation at the foot of the gravestone and anchored it with a little stone. "Daddy, this is Douglas, who I am going to marry. We want you to be at the wedding. I hope I will lead my life with Douglas in a way that will make you proud of me. Please give us your blessing." Tears came to Addy's eyes, and she prodded Douglas. "Say something."

Douglas hesitated and then saw that Addy was crying. He looked down and said, "I'm sorry that I never met you, sir, and I'll try to take good care of your daughter." He put his arm around Addy and pulled her to him. "Don't cry, Addy."

"You'll be my only friend, Douglas," Addy said and suddenly understood why her mother thought her brave. "I never thought about that before."

N.R. King

"I'll take care of you, Addy. I love you, and I want to take care of you for the rest of my life."

The trip to the cemetery left Addy feeling sad in the midst of all the activity in the house. She realized that she might never see her father's grave again, and, for the first time, began to think about other things she was leaving behind. When she took to spending hours in the garden alone, Bess scolded her.

"Just because you're the bride doesn't mean that you get to sit around while everybody else cooks and cleans and sews. Get in here right this minute, and do your share."

That cured Addy of any sorrow at leaving her mother's house. That and her suspicions about Rose. The more Rose helped with the wedding arrangements, the more Addy wondered about Rose's real motives. She couldn't believe Rose's good wishes and happy mood were entirely sincere and hoped they weren't simply a cover for more nighttime tea parties with Douglas.

As the wedding approached, the flurry of activity intensified to the point that Addy barely registered the arrival of Douglas's parents three days before the event. He brought them to the house for afternoon tea. It was a formal affair with Bess serving and Rose and Addy scurrying to carry out her orders. Douglas's mother seemed uncomfortable, and after laughing about the discomforts of their trip and attempting to hug Bess, she fell silent. Douglas's father, on the other hand, was talkative and showered Bess with compliments and his pleasure that Douglas had found such a lovely young bride to bring home. Bess calmly reigned over the ritual but seemed relieved when they left to spend the rest of their stay at the home of one of Douglas's professors. Addy was relieved, too. Dealing with a new mother-in-law and her loud laughter was more than she could face, though she thought Douglas's father seemed nice enough.

Douglas spent the next three days sightseeing with his parents and keeping them away from Bess's house.

At last the wedding day arrived, and everybody agreed that no bride ever looked more beautiful or groom more handsome as they stood together under the wedding canopy.

Addy answered when prompted by the rabbi but otherwise let her thoughts drift. She didn't want to think about the ceremony, but she couldn't prevent its consequence from springing to mind. She was about to follow this man across the ocean and live with him for the rest of her life. Though she knew she was supposed to keep her eyes demurely down, Addy peeked out the corner of her veil and saw Douglas peeking out of the corner of his eyes at her. Their eyes met for an instant, and though he tried to appear solemn, Addy saw that Douglas was working strenuously to suppress a smile that threatened to become a grin, maybe even a chuckle. She almost laughed out loud. Of course, this was the man for her. Of course, she was going to the States with him.

The dinner that followed the wedding added to Bess's reputation as a good cook, and proved her to be a gracious hostess, as well. Addy had never seen her mother so relaxed and outgoing. The only event missing from the reception was the traditional dance between the father of the bride and his daughter. At that moment, Addy missed her father more than she ever had before.

"Come, my dear," Max said as he approached her, "I don't want you to miss this moment. Let me be your father and celebrate my new daughter with a dance." He reached out

N.R. King

his hand and, as Addy took it, he swept her into his arms and began to move them to the music.

Before they had made one circuit of the dance floor, Douglas tapped his father's shoulder. "Give me my bride," he said.

"I'm taking the place of her father who can't be here. Don't make her miss this dance."

"You won't be taking anybody's place, and you won't be dancing with my wife. Don't try it again."

Douglas led Addy off the dance floor and sat with her at the head table. "Stay away from my father, Addy. You have no idea what he's capable of."

There was no point in arguing, but Addy couldn't see the harm of one dance with her father-in-law.

A week-long whirlwind of celebration and farewells followed the wedding. It was exhausting, and Addy found herself looking forward to the end of the festivities.

The night before they left for the States, Douglas went out with his friend, Nat, and Addy went to her bedroom to pack the rest of her clothing and possessions. Bess came in to help her.

"You leave tomorrow, Addy." Addy nodded and continued folding the last of her blouses. "Rose and I will miss you, but there's no sense in talking about that. You'll be safe across the ocean, and that will give us peace of mind. Be sure to write often, and let us know how you are. Send us snapshots, too, so we can see where you live."

"I'll write whenever I can."

Bess sat on the corner of the bed and smoothed her skirt. "Don't forget us, Addy. When I left Russia, the whole family scattered, and I never found out what happened to most of them. I still think about my sister, Faigel, and wish I had seen her again."

"Don't worry, Mama. I won't forget you, and I'll be fine. You know Douglas will take good care of me."

"I don't think I could send you with anybody else."

"You aren't sending me. I'm choosing to go."

"I know your father would have loved Douglas like a son." Bess was quiet as she unfolded the blouse Addy had just put in the suitcase and folded it again.

"You can do this, Addy. I did it, and you can do it, too. You're strong and sensible like me, and you know better than to let anybody see you as weak."

Addy was surprised to hear that her mother thought her sensible.

There was a long pause before Bess continued. "You can always come back, if you need to."

Addy was so shocked she almost laughed. What could possibly impel her to return? "I know, but I can't imagine anything would bring me back…for more than a visit," she hastily added, although she didn't plan to visit, either.

Bess seemed relieved by her answer.

"One more thing you almost forgot," Rose said as she came into the room carrying a square of gingham and Addy's old copy of *The Treasure Book of Fairytales*, its pages stuffed with Addy's collection of scraps. "You can't leave everything of your childhood behind, and one day you might have a little girl who will love arranging your scraps on the parlor rug just like you did when you were a little girl." Rose wrapped the book in the fabric and tied it with a bit of ribbon. "I don't want it to get damaged," she said. "Now it's ready to pack."

Addy hadn't planned to take that book with her, but she didn't object when Rose put it in her suitcase.

THE NEXT DAY, THE WHOLE FAMILY WENT TO WAVERLY STA-
tion. They had to hire a taxi because of all the luggage. Max,
Clara, Douglas, and Addy would be traveling first by train,
and then by ship to the States. Bess and Rose came to see
them off on the first leg of their journey.

After they were settled in their compartment, there were
hugs all around and kisses and tears from Bess.

"You'll be safe, Addy, and that's all I've wanted. For you to be
safe and happy," she said, wiping her tears and blowing her nose.

Not quite true, Addy suddenly realized. We've each done
our part. I'm leaving to be safe far away, and Rose is staying
to keep you and the shop safe at home. For an instant, Addy
wondered which of her daughters her mother had chosen to
protect, and which she had sacrificed.

When the whistle blew, Bess and Rose hurried off the
train. Addy looked out the window. Three soldiers stood
against a post, and an old lady carrying two bundles hurried
along the platform. Bess was crying and leaning against Rose,
who smiled broadly and waved. Addy knew she might never
see them again, and unexpected tears filled her eyes. But that
moment passed quickly. She was happy to be leaving, to be
the one setting off, not the one left behind. Isn't this what she
had always dreamed of? She couldn't wait to tell her story to
people who hadn't been there. And fix it.

After the War

1947

ROSE WAS FORTY YEARS OLD WHEN SHE SCANDALIZED THE neighborhood by becoming visibly pregnant. The Jewish community in Edinburgh was small and close-knit, and word spread quickly. Heads, tongues, and fingers wagged until all agreed that it was a good thing, after all, that her mother hadn't lived to see this terrible consequence of losing a father while still a child and growing up without a male in the household to protect a young girl's honor. Though Rose could hardly be called a young girl. In the past, they had called her our poor, dear Rose, but now they didn't know what to call her.

How could this have happened to Rose? Their own plain, sensible Rose. And why wasn't she the least bit upset and ashamed? How could she seem absolutely buoyant? And most important, of course, who was the father?

There was also the issue of whether or not they should still purchase their gloves, buttons, and ribbon from Rose. Everybody acknowledged that she had a lovely shop and stocked all the things they wanted, nothing too flashy or forward, nothing too expensive or obvious. Rose always knew what looked good and loved a little chat while she counted out your change. And Annie Epsin, the girl she had helping her, was as nice as she could be. But now? What could you chat about with her belly bulging between the two of you?

N.R. King

IN THE YEARS SINCE HER MOTHER'S DEATH, ROSE'S LIFE HAD settled into a predictable pattern. She shared her house with Nora, a war widow who rented a bedroom and worked as a seamstress out of the upstairs parlor. They enjoyed picture shows with friends and outings for tea and biscuits on Sunday afternoons. But nothing in her life was more important to Rose than her shop.

Before he died, Rose's father taught her everything she needed to know to manage the shop by herself. Even more, he taught her to love it the way he loved it. Rose enjoyed stocking the shelves, dressing the window, fixing the displays, and dealing with customers. She even liked doing the books in the evening and making the orders. Unpacking all the merchandise was like having a birthday every month, and setting it out for sale was like sharing her gifts. The salesmen who came by with sales pitches and samples of their wares admired her shrewd business sense and enjoyed her conversation. More than one had let her know that he would like to know her better. Nothing permanent, just good company now and again. But she knew better than to risk a fling with the likes of a salesman.

It pleased Rose to think that her father would be proud that she had gotten by, in spite of the war. Nobody knew how difficult it had been to sustain the shop when clothing was rationed and everybody was encouraged to mend and make do. Now that the end of the war promised a return to more prosperous times, Rose wondered why she wasn't happier. She missed her mother, of course, and her father who died so long ago, and her sister who lived in the States and wrote only occasionally. But it seemed that most of all, she missed the war.

Rose tried to banish that terrible suspicion from her mind, though she had to admit her pride in doing her part to save the world when she drew the blackout curtains every evening, woke to warning sirens and the roar of planes in the night, listened for the explosion of bombs and waited for the house to shake, and made do with what they grew in the backyard and what was left on the grocer's shelves. What could be that imperative or compelling again?

Then Rose met Thomas. He was a new salesman, a round man with ginger hair, bright green eyes, and a ruddy complexion. Older than the rest and quiet, he seemed at a loss to explain how he found himself selling bolts of cloth and seamstress supplies. Rose took pity on him and ordered more goods than usual, reasoning that Nora would use what the shop didn't sell.

Thomas stayed for a cup of tea in the back of the shop, and they shared bits of their lives during the war, the difficulties of travel, and the restlessness they both felt. Rose appreciated the thoughtful way he listened to her and his openness in sharing his own experiences. She liked the way he sat forward in his chair, smiling and holding his teacup, almost tenderly, in both hands while his eyes rested on her and a faint aroma of pipe tobacco escaped his vest pocket. He's an interesting man, she thought. A safe, comfortable man who makes me feel safe and comfortable and interesting, too. Before long, Thomas suggested that they share his mother's caravan, already parked by the sea, and spend a week refreshing themselves. Rose accepted.

It took a month to make the preparations. Rose invented a long-lost cousin on her mother's side who had miraculously survived the war and was reported to be in London. For good measure, she made her cousin alone and injured and then added that his entire family had been lost. Neighbors and customers clucked and fussed over poor, dear Rose, so ready and willing to visit a cousin she had never met.

With Annie to watch the shop and Nora to watch the house, Rose had no worries about leaving Edinburgh for a week. Her first trip set a precedent for traveling alone, and the neighbors became used to her setting off on little holidays now and again to see her cousin, who was doing quite well. In 1946 and 1947, Rose and Thomas made several week-long trips to refresh themselves by the sea, and nobody was the wiser.

Rose marveled at the way she and Thomas became old friends, almost immediately. From the first, there was no awkwardness between them. Thomas was a calm, gentle man, never at a loss for words and unfailingly interested in hearing Rose's thoughts. It surprised and then delighted her to find that he was also an eager and generous lover. She wondered where he had learned so much about women, but she didn't ask.

They enjoyed long walks along the beach and swam together every day. Thomas was an elegant swimmer and was pleased to find that Rose could keep pace.

"You're a grand girl, Rose," he said after one particularly long swim. "I've not met one like you before." And holding her face between his hands, he kissed her before they even got back to the caravan. A long kiss flavored with sea salt.

Though Thomas was Jewish, his parents hadn't kept any Jewish rituals or traditions, and he was not the least bit observant. Nonetheless, he agreed to make the blessings over the wine and the bread on Friday nights, repeating them word by word after Rose, and to refrain from smoking his pipe after dinner. That was all the Sabbath observance Rose expected of him, and Thomas seemed happy to comply.

In the fall of 1947, Thomas announced plans to emigrate to Australia in the spring. It seemed to Rose that she was not included, and as she thought it over, she realized that, even if invited, she would not leave the shop. A little adventure was one thing, but a change of hemispheres was something else, altogether.

Rose's holidays continued, though her cousin took a turn for the worse, and after a final trip at the beginning of March, she announced that her cousin had died while she was there, and it had been a peaceful end. The neighbors commiserated, and brought poor, dear Rose numerous casseroles and cakes to help her through this difficult time.

THE STOMACH VIRUS THAT STRUCK ROSE IN APRIL WAS worrisome and unpredictable. She was sickest in the mornings, but the nausea could overwhelm her at any time during the day. And rather than lasting a few days, this virus lingered. At Nora's urging, Rose made an appointment to see the doctor. She left the house for her doctor's appointment with a nasty virus and returned from his office six weeks pregnant.

Rose went to bed for the rest of the day, and Nora brought her tea and dry toast and didn't ask any questions. Rose asked herself plenty of questions, though. Starting with, how could this have happened to me at my age? Asked with a certain amount of pride and delight, she had to admit, and not one ounce of shame or regret. So what to do about the baby was answered. I'll have the baby, she told herself. And raise the child right here in Edinburgh.

When she thought about Thomas, the decisions became more complicated. He was a kind, well-meaning man, and she was sure he would take her to Australia with him if he knew about the baby. But abandon the shop? Impossible. The shop was left to me, she thought, and I've a duty to it. I don't want to go to Australia any more today than I did yesterday. The baby makes no difference. If I tell Thomas, he'll likely feel obligated to stay here. Unless I find some way of telling him while making it clear that his plans need not change. That will be difficult. So maybe I won't tell him at all and make it possible for him to do what his heart is set on. Or would that be stealing his child?

Rose hadn't reached any decision by the next morning. If anything, her thinking had become more muddled. Thomas planned to leave for Australia in two weeks and to stop by the shop for a "quick goodbye," as he had put it, before he left. By then she hoped she would know what to do.

It took Rose some time to keep down a cup of tea before leaving home, and Annie had already opened the shop before Rose got there. She was so late that two salesmen had already arrived, Thomas and a tall, dark-haired man.

Rose felt flustered in spite of herself. "Thomas, what a surprise. This isn't a day Annie and I expected you."

"It's not my usual day, but this is a special occasion. I'm leaving for Australia soon, and I want to introduce you to Kevin. He'll be taking over for me and bringing you all the wonderful items that I used to bring." Then he added with special emphasis and a little blush, "Items for your shop."

"We had no idea you had such grand plans," Annie said. "I wish you all the best."

Rose quickly echoed her sentiments and added, "When, exactly, do you leave?"

"Immediately, actually. I don't leave for Australia until next week, but I'm straight off to the train station from here to see my mum and dad in Glasgow, and from there I'll be making the rounds of other family I'm leaving behind."

"Have you been planning this trip long?" Annie asked.

"More than a year. Ever since my sister and her husband emigrated and began pestering me to join them. They say it's a grand life there."

"And you never said a thing? You're a great one for secrets, Thomas!" Annie laughed and turned to Rose, "Isn't he though?"

Rose had to laugh, too, and agree that Thomas was a great one for secrets. Was this the quick good-bye, then? There wasn't enough time to decide what to do, let alone enough time to do it. Even before Rose could bring her thoughts together, she was in the midst of a flurry of good wishes and handshakes, and Thomas and Kevin were gone.

"That was a surprise," Annie said. "And speaking of surprises, I worried when you weren't the first to the shop this morning. I don't remember one other time when I had to open for the day. Are you still feeling ill? What did the doctor say?"

"He said there is nothing to worry about. I'll be fine."

That evening, Rose realized that she was pleased with the way things had worked out. Her relief convinced her that she hadn't wanted to tell Thomas about the baby and that she almost certainly would not have. Still, she didn't feel quite at peace with what had happened. Part of her felt selfish, like she had stolen the best of Thomas and sent the rest to Australia. And she suspected the day would come when the baby would ask questions. She'd have some explaining to do then. But not right now.

Life went on as usual for the next six weeks. Rose's illness subsided, and her customers began to remark that she looked particularly well now that she felt better and had begun to put on a little weight. The shop was also doing well, and Nora's business was doing so well that she decided to ignore her family's pleas to return home to Aberdeen.

"Edinburgh's my home," she told Rose. "Even though Philip's gone, I'm not leaving."

Now her stable and predictable life comforted Rose. She didn't feel any of the restlessness of the past two years. Perhaps, she thought, the coming shake-up makes a little quiet before the storm a welcome thing.

The promise of financial security, company in the house, and help at work made Rose a bit more expansive than usual, and she hired a woman to clean the house once a week and the shop every day. She also hired a gardener.

THE BACKYARD GARDEN WAS HER MOTHER'S PRIDE BEFORE her father died and her sister's project afterwards. It had been a beautiful place full of flowers, fruit, vegetables, and one majestic apple tree. There was also a charming rustic bench and chair that her father had built for her mother. But during the war, the flowers had been discarded to make room for more vegetables, and maximizing the yield had driven out aesthetic concerns. Nobody had paid the garden any attention for the past two years, and now it was a mess of old plants and mud.

Even though she had pleasant memories of the lovely garden it used to be, Rose would have felt like a spendthrift to hire a gardener just to have a pretty backyard. But one morning in the butcher shop, of all places, hiring a gardener presented itself as a good deed she could do for a suffering young man.

Nora had been buying their meat for several weeks because the sight of raw flesh and the odors of blood and sawdust made Rose's virus much worse. But one Monday afternoon, Rose felt well enough to shop, herself. Mr. Blum, the butcher, greeted her like an old friend.

"Rose, how nice to see you. Nora told me you were ill. I'm glad you are well enough to get out again," he said. "How can I help you today?"

"Two chickens, please. A lovely young one for roasting, and an old flavorful hen for soup." For a moment, Rose felt like an old hen, herself, and almost laughed because she was also flavorful. Then she added, "I don't need anything too big, since it's just Nora and me."

"I've just what you need," Mr. Blum said reaching for two chickens and beginning to wrap them. "This one's the youngster, and here's your old bird."

"How is your family, Mr. Blum? Well, I hope."

Mr. Blum shook his head. "My nephew's no better, and now he never leaves the house. Doesn't talk to anybody and won't work here anymore, even though he knows that all this is supposed to be his, one day." Mr. Blum wound string around the two bundles he had made. "Says nobody understands him, that being around people makes him nervous. All night he paces the house, and every day he sits and stares out the window while my sister cries in her bedroom."

Rose knew the story. Everybody did. Berel had gone off to war a happy, excited young man who worked hard as his uncle's assistant, liked nothing better than a good joke, and loved his new bride. He had returned strange and silent, and had moved back into his mother's house when his wife left him.

"Your father was always kind to Berel," Mr. Blum said as he tied off the string around Rose's packages and placed them on the counter. "Do you remember how they worked together building those little airplanes on Sunday mornings when Berel was just a boy?"

Rose did remember the boy Berel had been. He was her sister's age, eight years younger than Rose, and Rose recalled him as a happy child always ready with a smile and a laugh as he traveled the neighborhood with his hat askew and one shoe untied. She also had vivid memories of those Sunday mornings when her mother's kitchen filled with the pungent fragrances of glue and fresh wood and the voices of the young boy and the old man reading the directions aloud and deciding who would hold the wood in place and who would apply the glue. Each Sunday, everybody who was in the house when the little plane was finished gathered in the backyard to witness its first flight. She believed that Berel had taken the place of the son her father never had, and that her father had played the role of a favorite uncle.

"I didn't know he was still doing so poorly. I'm sorry to hear he's not any better," Rose said.

"If we could just find something for him to do."

That's when Rose thought of her garden. "He'd be doing me a great favor if he could put my backyard right," she said. "I'll pay for the supplies he needs, and he can work in it for as long as it takes. I won't be able to pay him much, but I'll give him something."

Mr. Blum smiled. "That's very kind of you. He's a careful boy, and he learns what he needs to when he takes an interest. I'll speak to him. I'll say he would be doing you a great favor because a lady of your age can't be mucking about on her knees in the mud."

Rose wasn't too pleased with his description of her, but she didn't challenge it. And apparently, it worked, because three days later Berel showed up at her house early in the morning. She was shocked at how he had changed. He was no longer a young man with his cap pushed back on his head and a ready smile. Now, a thin, sullen man stood at her door, his coat buttoned up to his neck and his hands jammed into its pockets. He looked down when he spoke and seemed both angry and afraid.

"My uncle tells me you need a gardener."

"That I do. The yard's a mess, and I've no time or skill to make it better."

"I'll do it if you tell me what you want done."

"That will be grand."

"Just bring the instructions to the butcher shop," he said.

After he had gone, Rose found several old diagrams her sister had used years before and a list of the seeds and plants that had been purchased then. She gave them to Mr. Blum but told him that the diagrams and lists were just suggestions and Berel could do what he liked to make the garden pretty again. She also said that Berel could start any time and take as long as he wanted, that he was welcome to use her old garden tools, and that he should leave a bill for her at the butcher shop each week.

"I hope you won't mind being our middle-man," Rose said. "It's the arrangement that seemed to make Berel most comfortable."

"Mind? Not a bit. It's a great kindness you're doing for Berel. After one look at him, nobody else gave him a chance. You're your father's daughter through and through."

Since she was doing a good deed, Rose didn't feel like a spendthrift, though having a gardener made her feel a bit posh. I've quite the odd little household, she thought. And it's about to become odder, yet.

ROSE DIDN'T MIND SURPRISING EVERYBODY ELSE, BUT SHE decided it was unfair to surprise Nora and Annie. So one evening at dinner, she told Nora about the baby, and the next morning in the shop, she told Annie that she was pregnant. Just like that. No explanations, no timidity, no beating around the bush. Just the fact of the matter plainly stated. They were surprised, astounded really, and then delighted when they saw how pleased she was. Nora pledged her support and said she hoped that Rose would let her share in the childcare. Annie said she would help out in the shop as much as needed when the baby was tiny, and that her mum would be happy to watch Rose's baby since she was already watching Annie's little ones. This baby will be raised by a committee of aunties, Rose thought. A fortunate child. A fortunate mum.

As her pregnancy progressed, there was the buzz and rumble and roar of the community to contend with, but that hardly breached Rose's good spirits. She sailed into each day, buoyant with the expectation of adventure. It was Nora and Annie who came in for more questioning than Rose did.

Customers in little knots of two or three would descend on Annie if Rose was having her lunch in the back. They whispered furtively, sniffing and looking out the corners of their eyes. What has she told you? What do you know? Who's the father? Does she really plan to raise it by herself? Right here in Edinburgh?

"What would you have her do?" Annie would ask.

Then the ladies would take their little packages and their change, disappointed that Annie didn't have more information, and answer, "At the least, she needn't look so happy."

Nora heard the same sort of questions. Ladies with skirts to be hemmed or dresses to be altered would remind Nora of the story of Candace who had to take her little boy and move to Manchester, and then there was the MacDonald girl left behind with twins by that nasty medical student, the one from New Jersey. She was sent to live with her aunt.

Nora said she hadn't known Candace or the MacDonald girl, but surely these teenagers had nothing in common with Rose, our own Rose. A grown woman, a sensible woman. Not as sensible as she thought she was, the ladies scoffed.

In spite of their scorn, the community thrived on Rose's pregnancy. They bonded around their quest for information, and Rose's apparent depravity elevated their appreciation of their own moral superiority. Nora's business and the shop thrived, too. And so did the garden.

Berel was reliable and hard-working, and Rose's garden slowly regained its former beauty. Colorful flowers ringed the base of the apple tree again, and a new bed of roses grew along one wall. The first time Rose came into the garden and spoke to him, Berel, startled by her voice, had jumped up and shouted in alarm. Then, embarrassed and angry, he had stomped off to the far corner of the garden where he had worked with his back to her until she went indoors. Since then, Rose was careful to stay on the stoop until Berel noticed her. Only then did she admire his handiwork. He always nodded in acknowledgment of her compliments, but he didn't reply.

Once, however, after Rose washed the garden tools and then forgot to return them to the outdoor shed Berel had built in the back corner of the yard, he had pounded on the kitchen door and even her apology was not enough to appease him.

"The things I need must be where I can find them. I'll wash them myself, or use them dirty, but I can't have them moved."

"You're quite right," Rose had said. "I'm sorry, and it won't happen again." She didn't point out that these were her tools and she could do what she wanted with them, or that it was rude and impolitic of him to be shouting at an employer. The vehemence of his response spoke more of other times than a sunny morning in Edinburgh and other places than her quiet garden. Rose couldn't understand those times and places, but she could recognize their hold on Berel.

As her pregnancy progressed, Rose began to go to the shop a bit later in the mornings and leave a bit earlier in the afternoons. Annie assured her that she didn't mind opening and closing and that tiring more easily was to be expected. Rose was surprised at how little she objected to being sent home early, and how pleasant a little extra sleep in the morning felt.

One day, when Rose noticed that the old bench and garden chair had been washed and repaired, she took her morning cup of tea outdoors and sat in the garden before going to the shop. Berel was already working, but they didn't speak. Rose also began taking her tea and her book out to the garden in the late afternoon. It relaxed her to sip and read or to watch Berel planting seeds outside while listening to the distant clatter of Nora's sewing machine stitching seams inside. She felt surrounded and protected, and a just bit indolent. She knew this wouldn't last long, and she didn't mind enjoying it for the moment. The shop may have finally met its match, she thought, and patted the mound of her belly. I wondered if I would ever love anything as much as I love the shop. Now that question seems to have been settled. But the best is that I'll have them both.

2

ONE MORNING AFTER EVERYBODY ELSE HAD KNOWN ABOUT Rose's pregnancy for some weeks, Berel seemed to become aware of it for the first time and rushed to the steps to take her tea from her hand and help her to the garden chair. Rose laughed and said she didn't need a hand, but she let him carry her cup and saucer. She put her book on the bench while she took her tea from him, and saw Berel look at the title.

"Reading *The Moonstone*, are you?" he said.

Rose didn't know if she was more dismayed by the sound of his voice, or by his question. "Have you read it?" she asked.

"I have," Berel said. He smiled and a little chuckle escaped him. "Don't sound so surprised."

A smile and a small laugh were almost more than Rose could believe. "I bet your old mates would be surprised, too."

"I have no old mates, but if I had any, they would be surprised. I never let on to anybody that I like to read. Wouldn't have helped my image, now, would it? So how far along in the story are you? Has the diamond been stolen yet?"

"Yes, the diamond is missing. And I think it's been hidden by Rachel."

Berel smiled and looked mysterious. "Keep reading."

After that, Rose was expected to report each morning about her reading of the day before. Rachel hadn't taken the diamond, and neither had any of Rose's other suspects. When suspicion fell on Franklin, Rose didn't believe it.

"I've been led astray so many times that I refuse to fall for any more false clues," she said.

"So how do you explain the evidence?" Berel asked.

"I can't. But I don't believe it."

"Now you are cultivating a superiority to reason," Berel said. "Just like Sergeant Cuff."

"That I am," said Rose and laughed. "It may be a trait I've had for some time."

"I'm trying to cultivate that trait, myself," Berel said.

When Rose finished reading *The Moonstone*, Berel asked her to name her favorite character. While she was thinking, he said that he liked Sergeant Cuff best.

"That's interesting," she said, "I also like one of the secondary characters best. I like Miss Clock."

"Miss Clock? The fussy, nosey old maid?"

"Yes. I thought she was funny. But just because I liked her best in the story, doesn't mean I wish I had a Miss Clock in my life, listening at doors and leaving uplifting tracts about the house." Rose laughed and then looked sharply at Berel. "Be careful what you say about old maids."

Berel blushed. "I didn't mean any insult," he stammered. When he saw that Rose was laughing again, he smiled broadly. "I hadn't recognized you as a tease, Rose." And then added, "Miss Clock would never condone teasing."

The first time he's joined in a joke and the first time he's used my name, Rose thought. I do believe he's recovering from the war.

When Rose's next-door neighbor peered over her fence one day to admire the garden, Rose was quick to credit Berel. The day after, the neighbor came into the yard to ask Berel if he would also look after her garden. Rose was pleased to hear him accept the second job, and she told him that he was welcome to use her garden tools in her neighbor's yard.

"I won't be giving your yard any less than it needs," he assured her. "But there's time to clean her yard, too."

"I've no worries of being neglected, and I'm glad you have a second garden to look after."

"I think I'm meant to be a gardener," he said. "It's better than cutting up dead animals."

Berel's mood continued to lighten. He smiled, joked, and

began to seem more like a mature version of the boy he had been than the old man who had returned from the war.

When Rose began a new book, *Titus Groan*, Berel commented that he hadn't read this one.

"It's new," she said. "Very odd, but interesting."

"I think I'll get a copy," he said.

Each morning, Rose and Berel chatted in the garden before she went to the shop. Sometimes about books, sometimes about the weather, sometimes about the garden. Never about the baby. Never about the war.

THE DOCTOR CALLED ROSE'S PREGNANCY NORMAL AND uneventful. Uneventful? The physical changes were immense. At one point, she feared the arrival of twins, but the doctor assured her that there was just one heartbeat, strong, steady and quite loud, but just one. As significant and obvious as the physical changes were, they were easily matched by less obvious but no less profound emotional changes. Rose sometimes felt like a great ship carrying hidden treasure, and, at other times, like a vessel commandeered by a tyrant. Sometimes she felt invulnerable, sailing across streets without looking both ways and smiling at strangers. At other times, she felt anxious and worried about nothing at all. All normal, Annie reassured her. Nothing to worry about.

The closer the arrival of the new baby, the more accustomed the women of the community grew to Rose's condition and the more their curiosity and disdain mellowed until they devised a new theory. She was not a depraved woman, after all. She was the victim of an unscrupulous character who had bewitched and then abandoned her. Rose found the latest rendition of her story no less insulting and feared that if there were an unscrupulous character in the story, she, herself, was the most likely candidate.

Well into the fall, Berel continued to work in the garden, and though he had several other gardens to look after, he was always at Rose's house in the early morning wearing an old jacket with the collar open and one sleeve rolled up while the other flapped around his wrist. Even if it was cool, Rose would slip on a jumper and go outside so they could chat while she sipped her tea and he worked. If it was too chilly and she saw him through the window, Rose sometimes called Berel into the kitchen, and they sat together at the table for a cup of tea. Nora often came downstairs and joined them. It pleased Rose to see Berel look relaxed and almost happy, and she began to wonder if there might be some attraction between him and Nora.

One morning, Rose and Berel found themselves alone at the kitchen table. Nora had gone shopping and wasn't expected back until lunch. Rose had planned to leave for the shop long before Nora went out, but she had had trouble falling asleep the night before and had overslept.

"How are you feeling, Rose?" Berel asked.

Rose was surprised by so personal a question. "Well, thank you," she responded.

"I've been thinking about your baby."

Rose nodded but had no idea how to respond.

"What's the little one going to do for a father?"

That would be a bold statement for anyone to make, but coming from Berel, it was both outrageous and touching.

"The baby will be fine," Rose said. "I'll make sure of that."

"But you can't be its dad."

"It will grow up with all the love it needs."

"I could be the dad," Berel said.

Rose was astonished and still searching for a way to tell him that his suggestion was absurd without insulting him when he rushed on.

"I see you're surprised, but I've thought this through. You must admit we get along, and even though you might think we don't love each other, we would both love the wee one. That would be enough to make us a family."

"But, Berel, you're not the dad."

"Nobody need know that."

"I'd be considered a temptress, and you'd be considered a rogue."

"I'd rather they thought me a rogue than what they think me now. And the blame would be all mine. They would think you kindly. And that's just what you are."

Rose shook her head. "But…"

Berel interrupted her. "Don't say anything else right now. Think about it." He put his cup down. "Try to cultivate a Sergeant Cuff attitude. A superiority to reason. We won't say one word about this for a week while you think."

After Berel left, Rose sat for some time at the table by herself. It's all well and good to invoke Sergeant Cuff, but what would Miss Clock say?

ROSE DID THINK ABOUT IT. HER FIRST REACTION WAS TO reject Berel's suggestion as preposterous. She was so much older. She didn't love him or think of him in a husband sort of way. He wasn't the baby's father. Still, it was true that they got along together, and she believed he was sincere in promising to be a loving father and a good husband. But those weren't reasons enough to marry him.

At the end of the week and in spite of the hours she had spent considering Berel's proposal, Rose's initial rejection remained her position. It seems that I want the baby, she thought, but I don't want a husband even when given the chance. So I can't marry Berel, and I have to make him understand that. And she did. Kindly, she hoped, but clearly.

"I was afraid that's what you would say," Berel said. "Maybe I went about this all wrong. Maybe I should have romanced you, and shown you that a marriage between us would be loving and good. I don't think my mum and dad love each other, but they have a peaceful life."

"Berel, we aren't suited to be more than friends. I enjoy your company, and I'm grateful for your friendship, but it won't ever be more than that. Lift your eyes a little, and you'll see young women much better suited to you than I am."

It seemed that Berel accepted defeat until two weeks later, when he surprised Rose again.

"I understand that you don't want to marry me, Rose," he said, sitting on the garden bench next to her chair. He fumbled with his collar for a moment and tugged at the front of his shirt. "You don't love me, and you're older than I am. These things don't matter to me, but I understand that they matter to you. Now think about this. Even if we don't marry, you could name me as the father of the baby. I would take responsibility for the child and help you every way I can, and the baby would get my insurance money one day. Think about that. Just because you don't want me as a husband, the baby doesn't have to be fatherless."

Rose was too astounded to reply.

"Don't say anything," Berel continued. "I can see you're surprised, so think as long as you like. I won't speak of this again until you do."

Though Rose could understand Berel's desperation for someone to love and call his own, she knew she couldn't give him another man's child. Wouldn't unmarried parents be worse in the eyes of the community than no father at all? And who would believe it? She certainly didn't find it believable, and she was sure the baby wouldn't believe it, either. The baby could have only one father, and that one couldn't be based on a lie, no matter how well intentioned.

The morning Rose planned to talk to Berel brought a downpour heavy enough to keep him out of the garden. Rose finished her breakfast alone and was clearing her dishes from the table when the front doorbell rang. Berel had come to the front? Not likely. But a visitor? At this hour? In this weather? How odd.

When Rose answered the door, she found Berel's mother standing under a dripping umbrella, looking grim. Had something happened to Berel?

"What a surprise. Come in out of the storm," Rose said, hurrying her visitor in and closing the door against the driving rain. She put the umbrella in the stand and hung the dripping coat on the clothes tree. "Take off your wet shoes, and I'll be back in a jiff with warm slippers."

Rose settled Berel's mother in the parlor with tea and biscuits before daring to speak of anything more than the dismal weather.

"Lovely of you to stop by, Mrs. Gerstein. I'm sorry it's raining too hard for me to show you what Berel has accomplished in my garden. He's all right, isn't he?"

"Rose, dear, you must call me Frieda. We're nearly the same age, so there's no need to call me Mrs. Gerstein."

The same age? Rose felt the implied insult.

"Let me come right to the point of my visit," Mrs. Gerstein continued. "Berel tells me he's the father of your child, or, at least, you are going to claim that he is." Mrs. Gerstein sipped her tea while she waited for the impact of her statement to

N.R. King

sink in before she continued. "It's an outrageous suggestion, of course, and nobody will believe it. I'm sorry that you find yourself alone with this predicament, but it would be wrong of you to involve Berel."

Rose bit her lip and took a deep breath in an effort to hold her tongue. How could anyone call her baby a predicament? How could a mother meddle in her grown son's life? Rose vowed to remember this moment and bring it to mind any time she felt compelled to meddle in her own child's life. But that vow for the future, as comforting as it was, did not solve the immediate problem, the one sitting in her parlor.

"I hope what I've said has made an impression on you, Rose. Soon you will be a mother, yourself, and you'll realize how important it is to protect your child. That's the reason I'm here, to protect Berel."

"Berel is not a child. He doesn't need you to protect him from anybody, and he certainly doesn't need you to protect him from me."

"I'm glad to hear that. But are you really planning to name him as your child's father?"

"I think I should resolve that question with Berel before I talk about it with anyone else." Rose knew that taking on his mother would only complicate Berel's life as well as her own, and she silently congratulated herself on her diplomatic response, though she longed to make a more biting retort.

Mrs. Gerstein put her cup down and pushed the plate of biscuits away. "If you persist in involving him, I'll be forced to tell everyone that he had no part in your pregnancy. Who will set foot in your shop once they know you've told lies about Berel?"

"I don't tell lies."

"Then I trust you will leave Berel out of your story." She rose abruptly to leave. "It would be better if Berel does not learn about my visit this morning."

"I agree that it would be best if neither of us mentions this visit. You can be sure I will protect your confidence for Berel's sake."

Mrs. Gerstein put on her wet shoes and raincoat and retrieved her umbrella.

"One more thing," Rose said as she opened the front door. "Your visit will have no influence on whatever happens between Berel and me."

With Berel's mother gone, Rose wandered back to the parlor and sat heavily in the big winged chair next to the plate of biscuits. She had to admit that what she witnessed this morning could be explained as a demonstration of Mrs. Gerstein's concern for Berel, however wrongheaded and cruel her behavior. Only the threat to the shop frightened Rose. The business had weathered the first reaction to her pregnancy, but would it weather another assault? Sacrificing the shop for the baby seemed just as impossible as sacrificing the baby for the shop had seemed. No need to choose, Rose reminded herself. I've already decided to reject Berel's offer. And, as hard as it is to admit, for some of the very reasons his mother raised.

Rose's hand reached for another biscuit and felt the empty plate. All the biscuits? I've eaten all the biscuits. Rose laughed out loud and heaved herself out of the chair. Time to go to the shop. I'm so late today that Annie will think I've slipped and drowned in a puddle, not knowing that the great balloon of my belly would keep me afloat.

WHEN ROSE ARRIVED AT THE SHOP, ANNIE RUSHED TO HELP her with her raincoat and take her umbrella from her. "I wondered what had become of you. I've got the kettle on for a nice cup of hot tea, and you can rest at the back as long as you like. We won't be busy today, and I almost called to let you know you could stay home."

"Annie, you are a dear. I will have a bit of tea, and I'll use the day to make our orders. We can do that together. It's time you learned how."

"I don't want to make orders. I love being out front with the customers." Annie hesitated before continuing. "But I know somebody who would be eager to learn."

Rose was not surprised that Annie had no interest in the ordering, but she was surprised that Annie had somebody else to suggest.

"It's my husband," Annie said.

"Henry is interested?"

"Yes. He's working for that trucking company he was with before the war, but he says there's no future there. I'm always going on and on about how lovely the shop is, and he says he has ideas about how it could grow."

"Grow?"

"Well, not get bigger, exactly. Henry says you could expand what you do. He thinks you could keep the shop going the way it is while you do more trade with the tailors and the seamstresses. You could order for them the way you do for Nora, and he could deliver to them and take their new orders. Could he come to the shop one day and talk to you about his ideas?"

"He'd better do it before the baby comes and we're all distracted," Rose said.

That night in bed, Rose thought back over her interesting day. I love my little shop, she thought. I love it just the way it is, just the way Papa left it for me. What would he do? Rose smiled. He would let it grow. Especially since Henry's idea sounds like a good one. Nothing ventured, nothing gained. That's what he would say. Or some pithy Yiddish equivalent. And it's really Henry taking the risk, though it will be up to me to help him succeed.

Then her thoughts drifted toward the other interesting part of her day, Mrs. Gerstein's visit. Rose sighed. There's only one right decision about the baby's father. The pity is that she will think I was intimidated and she was right in coming here. That will be the sorry consequence of doing the right thing. Papa would probably have had a saying for that, too.

THE NEXT DAY WAS BRIGHT AND SUNNY, AND BEREL CAME into the garden full of good cheer. Rose was already sitting in her garden chair with her usual cup of tea.

"A lovely day, isn't it, Rose?"

"A sight better than yesterday," she answered and sat for a long time sipping her tea and watching Berel dig with a trowel along the back fence. A tray of small plants waited next to him.

"I'm pleased that you want to help with the baby," she finally said. "And I know you'll be a wonderful influence on the child. But I can't lie and say that you are the father. That's not fair to any of us."

"You didn't think long," Berel called out. "Why hurry such an important decision?"

Rose watched him dig beautifully symmetrical holes, one for each tiny plant.

"I don't need more time," she said. "This is the best decision for everybody. One day, Berel, you will marry and have children of your own."

Berel stood and stared at her. "This isn't about me. It's

about your baby that needs a father."

"It's about what's best for all of us. It's about…"

"Are you saying that no father at all is better than me?" Berel shouted. "That I'm not even better than nobody?"

"No, Berel," Rose answered as quietly as she could. "You would be a father any child would be lucky to have. But this baby can't begin life with a lie."

Berel stood and threw the trowel into the dirt. "And where is the father?" he yelled, wiping his hands on his shirt and moving toward her. "What kind of man abandons the woman who is carrying his child? Is that the kind of father you want your baby to have?"

It shocked Rose to hear Thomas so maligned. A more unfair accusation could not be imagined, and she almost defended him. But she couldn't admit to Berel that she had hidden the baby from its father. That even if she wouldn't let Berel steal the child, she had already stolen it.

When she didn't reply, Berel closed his eyes and took a deep breath. "Rose, you look so pale. I didn't mean to frighten you. I'm sorry. It's only my disappointment speaking." He pulled at his shirt and ran his fingers through his hair. "I know you've the right to make any decision you think best."

His sudden sadness and remorse got the better of her, and Rose began to cry.

"Oh, no, first I frightened you, and now I've made you cry. Don't be sad, Rose. Please forgive me." Berel sat on the bench and looked out across the garden. "I won't ever speak like that again. The question is behind us. Only cheer up."

Rose smiled at him. "Thank you, Berel. There are few in my life who are as good to me as you are. I'll be proud and grateful to have you as part of the child's life. You could be its only uncle. There's no one else to fill that place, and I'd be happy if you would."

Berel grinned at her. "What a lovely idea, Rose. Thank you. I accept with pleasure. I'll love the little thing as only an uncle can and think myself lucky. Your father was like an uncle to me, and now I'll be an uncle to his grandchild."

"The baby will be lucky, too, Berel," Rose said, relieved that he had accepted her decision without more drama.

That night in bed Rose tallied the baby's family. One mum, that's me, two aunties, Nora and Annie, one great-auntie, Annie's mum, two cousins, Annie's little ones, and now an uncle, as well. That's more family than I ever had. There's also an aunt and an uncle and two cousins in the States, but they don't know about the baby. I'll tell them when it's born. Only Thomas is absolutely missing. I don't even know how to find him. But that's not a problem since I've no plans to tell him anyway.

3

Josephine Beatrice Kaminsky, to be known as Josie, appeared in the early morning on November 30, 1948. She was a fine, lusty baby who cried mightily when hungry or uncomfortable, and audibly sighed after a satisfying burp or as she fell asleep. She peered about from the very first, and soon had all the principals in her life categorized and understood. Then she relaxed and agreed to be loved and to love in return.

When Josie was only a few hours old, Rose was surprised to see the little thing staring back at her with the same intensity she felt while examining the tiny face. The rosy complexion was from Thomas, as were the green eyes and reddish hair. In fact, all of Josie's pretty little baby features were from her father, and Rose worried that somebody might recognize him in her. She needn't have worried. Thomas had been an infrequently seen salesman, with no known connection to Rose. It helped that he had been in Australia for almost a year, and by now, nobody gave him a second thought. Except Rose, now and again.

Rose rested in the maternal hospital for a week and then brought Josie home in a taxi. Nora met them at the door. She had been to visit at the hospital, of course, but welcoming Josie home was still an occasion, and she had been careful not to schedule any appointments that morning.

Nora wasn't the only person at the house to welcome Rose and the baby. Berel was there, too, and Rose was a little surprised to see him. They had had a bit of a tiff the week before when he came to visit her and the nurse announced that Josie's father was here to see the baby. Rose had had a moment of confusion wondering how Thomas could possibly be visiting. Then Berel had walked in carrying a bouquet of roses.

"Berel," Rose had said, with some relief and more than a little irritation. "Whatever made the nurse think you are Josie's father?"

"That's what I told her," he answered.

"Why did you do that? You aren't the baby's father, and we agreed that you can't pose as her father, either. Don't you remember?"

"Of course, I remember. But I was afraid they wouldn't let just any man in, and it seemed a harmless enough fib. I am to be her favorite uncle, after all."

They both stopped talking when the nurse bustled in with a vase for the flowers and set it on the window ledge.

"Lovely," she said as she arranged the bouquet. "And a perfect choice for the mother," she added, winking at Berel. "Here's a thoughtful dad for you."

The extravagance of the flowers annoyed Rose as much as the extravagance of Berel's claims of fatherhood, but this was not the time or place for an argument. Since the day he had yelled at her in the garden, Berel had been cheerful and kind, and it did her good to see him happy. Rose had no desire to quarrel with him again.

When the nurse was safely out of the room, Berel said, "I stopped by the nursery to see the baby, and she's quite the pretty little Scot. You should have named her Bonnie."

Berel had never asked the identity of the father, and Rose wondered if he was fishing for information now. It won't do him any good, she thought. That secret is safe until the day that Josie asks, and forever, if she doesn't.

"She's named for my parents," Rose said. "The only baby who is."

"I know. And it's a lovely name. She makes a perfect little Josie."

Their conversation turned to news of the neighborhood and the work Berel was doing in her garden and in the other gardens he cared for. When he left, Rose worried about the role he hoped to play in Josie's life.

Now Rose nodded to Berel as she stepped into the foyer and handed the little bundle to Nora while she took off her coat. By the time she turned back, it was Berel who was holding the baby and unwrapping her. He peeled back the layers gently and laughed when he saw the baby's face. Nora laughed, too.

"She's giving you the once over," Nora said. "Having quite the good look at you. I hope she approves." At the sound of

Nora's voice, the baby turned her head. "Oh, so now it's my turn. Well, you're looking at your Auntie Nora. Not a real auntie, but one who will love you like a real auntie just the same, and help your mum take care of you. Don't worry about a thing. We've a whole family lined up for you." Nora took the baby from Berel's lap and gave her back to Rose. "We're all of us happy for you and happy for Josie and happy to be part of all this." She dabbed her eyes. "Now to show the little princess to her room, and then we'll have a cup of tea and relax."

Everybody trooped upstairs to the room that had been set aside for the nursery, a room that Rose and Nora had painted a neutral cream color and outfitted in curtains and pillows suited for either a boy or a girl. Though now that Josie was here, it was impossible to believe that anybody else had been expected. Rose was surprised that the door was closed. Nobody moved to open it, so Rose opened the door, herself, and walked in with Berel and Nora behind her.

The baby didn't seem alarmed by the room, but Rose was shocked. Josie had come home to a pastel pink room, and a pink crib with a newly crocheted pink and white blanket on it, a pink rocker with pink pillows on a pink oval rug, and pink curtains with little frills and flounces covering the windows. In fact, the room was quite relentlessly pink. Rose gasped as she came in.

"See," Berel said to Nora. "I told you she would love it. Pink is perfect for little girls."

"We can tone it down if it's a bit much," Nora said.

"It's not too much," Berel said. "It's perfect. Am I right, Rose?"

Rose rested Josie in her crib and covered her with the blanket before answering. "You are right, Berel. This room shows Josie how much she is loved, and how can any baby be loved too much?"

Josie marked her assent by sighing and closing her eyes.

That evening Rose and Nora sat together for a cup of tea before bed.

"I hope Josie's room wasn't too great a shock for you," Nora said. "Once Berel gets an idea into his head, he's very hard to dissuade."

"I can't say I wasn't surprised. But I know it was Berel's way of caring for us. He needs to feel like he's part of the family."

"But there's times he won't listen without getting angry, and then he scares me."

"Berel's still troubled by the war, but he'd never do us any harm. I still think about the jolly young man he used to be, and I've not given up the hope that he'll be that young man again."

AT EIGHT WEEKS, JOSIE WAS LOUD AND DEMANDING WHEN AWAKE, smiling and gurgling to anybody who crossed her line of vision, and impatient if hungry or if she had nobody to talk to. Rose found it best to keep the baby next to her no matter what she was doing. Then Josie was happy to comment on events without actually intruding. The baby usually watched dinner preparations and sometimes watched Nora sew or her mother knit. She liked to be held up to the window and watch Berel in the garden where, in spite of the cold, he said there was work to be done.

If it was particularly bright and sunny, Rose wrapped Josie in her big pink and white blanket and took her out to the garden where the two of them sat in the garden chair and watched Berel work. One afternoon a large wood pigeon landed on the back of their chair and surveyed the garden with them.

"Your ladyship," Berel said, bowing low to the ground. "I see that you and Titus are joined by one of your feathered friends this morning."

"You've read *Titus Groan*," Rose said, delighted to join the game. She had so little time to read these days that she had forgotten what a pleasure it was to talk about books.

"I have, and though you aren't a huge fat lady, you'll do for the Countess, and, though Josie's not an ugly baby boy, she's the only one who can play the part of Titus in a convincing manner. At least the bird is really a great big bird," Berel said.

Rose considered the rest of the characters. "There aren't any good choices for the others. I suppose Nora might agree to be Lady Fuchsia even though she's not an adolescent given to bizarre behavior. It's Annie's mum who must be Nannie Slagg, seeing as she cares for the children. That leaves you, Berel. Who are you?"

Berel didn't answer immediately, and Rose thought he had tired of the game.

"I suppose I'm a bit of all the men. I can't be Lord Sepulchrave, though he and I share a melancholy nature and love of reading, because I'm not the father of the child. And I don't hope for his fate since I don't want to become insane and believe I'm an owl. I don't want to be Steerpike who comes to overthrow and destroy everything. I think I must be Mr. Flay, the faithful servant who wants only to protect and preserve."

"That's a nice way of saying he's the guardian of convention and conformity. I'm not sure you qualify." Rose laughed. "We're hardly living a conventional life."

Berel laughed, too. "That's not quite true. We've just redefined what passes for conventional, and now I protect it."

Later Rose wondered what he meant and hoped he wasn't too serious about his role. Who did he think he was protecting their little family from? And did he feel as bound to her and Josie as Mr. Flay was bound to the Countess and

Titus. Rose hoped not.

⤞⤏⤙⤚⤚⤚⤟⤞⤞⤞⤍

EVERYBODY IN JOSIE'S FAMILY, EVEN ANNIE'S MUM WHO
had cared for many babies over the years, agreed that Josie
was precocious. They were most impressed by the fact that she
slept through the night before she was six weeks old. Brilliant,
they all agreed, to have figured out the difference between
night and day at such an early age.

Not only Annie's mum, but the ladies of the community,
as well, were won over by stories of Josie's accomplishments,
and they all wanted to see her. When they came to the house
for fittings, Nora was careful to keep Josie out of sight. If they
wanted a look at the baby, they would have to call on Rose
like civilized people. And they did want a look at the baby.

So Rose found herself having visitors in little groups of
two and three. They came with casseroles because a household
with a new baby has no time to cook, and they came with
little handmade dresses and caps and jackets because even a
little baby needs lovely things to wear. Peace offerings, Rose
thought. The price of a peek at the baby and a guess about
her father, Nora believed.

"Such a pretty name," the ladies would say. "Perfect for
such a pretty baby." Then they would study her features
and return her to Rose and wish her well before leaving and
reconvening for another cup of tea in a different parlor. Lovely
baby was the consensus. But she doesn't look anything like
dear Rose, or like anybody in Rose's family. She must look
like her father. Not that we recognize anybody in her. At
least she doesn't look like Berel, and that's a relief to Frieda.
Remember when he was saying he was the dad?

Berel took his role as Josie's uncle seriously. Whenever it

was warm enough, he came by to take her out for a stroll in her carriage. At first, Rose had been reluctant to let Berel take Josie out on his own. She had seen moments in the past when he wasn't quite in control of himself, and she didn't want him to endanger Josie. But the more Rose watched them together in the house, the less she worried. Even if the baby cried, Berel was patient. Nothing Josie did flustered him. Eventually, Rose agreed to let the two of them walk around the neighborhood with the understanding that he would come straight home if Josie started to fuss.

The morning of their first walk, Rose watched them set off, Josie barely visible in her bundle of blankets and Berel with his cap pushed back on his head, smiling broadly. He's beginning to look like the little boy Papa loved, Rose thought. Time and patience are all he needs. How can we deny him that?

Rose also warned Berel not to let his business suffer, but he assured her that there was time for everything, that he was Josie's only uncle, that they were good for each other. Rose couldn't dispute any of that. It did appear that his garden business was doing well, so well that he had even bought himself an old car. And it did seem that they were good for each other. Josie went quite wild at the sight of him, and he mellowed at the sight of her. In fact, it seemed to Rose, they were all good for each other.

FRIDAY NIGHT DINNER WAS ALWAYS A LITTLE SPECIAL FOR Rose and Nora. Rose roasted a chicken and baked a cake, and Nora made a potato kugel and vegetables. But they hadn't ever done more than that. It was Berel's idea to make it a real Shabbos meal.

"You should begin lighting Friday night candles like your mother did," he told Rose. "You're a mother now, yourself, and Josie should grow up in a house that has Shabbos candles."

"Rose," Nora cautioned when she heard the plans for Shabbos dinners, "you shouldn't let Berel tell you what to do."

"But neither should I dismiss a good idea just because Berel suggested it."

Nora had no answer to that.

Berel brought wine and joined them every Friday night. The women lit their candles; Berel said the blessings over the wine; Josie commented on the proceedings; and they ate together. Just like a family, Rose thought, and tried to keep the image of Thomas from coming to mind. Kind, reliable Thomas. Running awkwardly on the beach, and then surprisingly graceful and sleek in the water. Where was he now?

ONE SUNDAY MORNING, WHILE JOSIE STILL SLEPT IN HER pink crib, Rose and Nora were enjoying a leisurely breakfast of omelets and toast. They had set out all the jam jars in the house and were having a taste of every one.

"I've met a man," Nora said. "And I think he's a nice man."

Rose spread some of the strawberry preserves on a bit of toast before responding. "It seems you must think him more than just nice, Nora, if you're bothering to mention him at breakfast." She looked up to see Nora blush and laughed. "There's a telling pink to your cheeks," she said. "Who is he? How did you meet him?"

"His name is Dennis Linkman, and he's a brother to Sarah Bentley. I've been letting out her skirts now that she's put on a bit of weight, and taking up the hems as well. That way she doesn't have to tell anybody about the letting out and can say she has me making them more fashionably short." Nora laughed. "I love the stories they tell each other."

"How did you meet Sarah's brother?"

"She asked me if I would meet him when he came to visit. He's never married and lives in Birmingham. She said he's very nice, so I agreed to let him take me to dinner."

"It seems you agree with his sister."

"I do. He's a nice man, and I enjoy going out with him. He doesn't mind that I'm a wee bit older than he is or that I've been married. Lately, he's been coming to see his sister nearly every week, and she told me not to make the mistake of thinking it's her he wants to see."

"I'm happy for you, Nora. He must be a good man if you've taken a liking to him."

"I'd love to have you meet him. Can I invite him to dinner on Friday night?"

"Of course. Guests are welcome anytime."

So much for a romance between Nora and Berel, Rose thought as she lifted Josie out of her crib later that morning. It would have been too neat and tidy, in any case. And might not have helped me feel less responsible for the two of them. "You're the only one I want to be responsible for," she told the baby.

On Friday night, Rose could see that Nora had taken special care in setting the table. There were even new cloth napkins to match a new tablecloth. The menu didn't change, of course, since anything but the traditional meal was unthinkable.

"You would think it had been handed to Moses on Mount Sinai," Thomas used to complain when Rose insisted on chicken and kugel every Friday night, even in the little caravan at the beach. Thomas, Rose mused. It must be Nora's bringing Dennis to dinner that's brought him to mind.

When Dennis arrived, it was clear that he had also taken special care. He was freshly shaved, and his hair was slicked back. His suit was pressed; his shoes were shined; and he carried a great bunch of flowers.

After the flowers were transferred to a vase and put on the dining room table, the three of them settled themselves in the parlor. Dennis was pleasant company, and the talk flowed easily from topic to topic. Rose could see why Nora liked him.

Berel came in some twenty minutes later. Rose had told him that there would be another person at dinner on Friday, but she hadn't elaborated. When she saw Berel's face as he looked at the little group in the parlor, she wished she had.

Berel had washed up a bit after his day in somebody's garden and changed his shirt, but he still had a rumpled look about him. The contrast with Dennis made him look more rumpled, yet. It seemed that he realized his disadvantage and buttoned his shirt collar and smoothed his hair as he strode into the room, immediately on the offensive.

"Who are you?" Berel demanded before either of the women could make an introduction.

Nora had never seen Berel like this, but Rose had, and she moved to prevent a show of temper if she could.

"Berel, I'm glad to see you," she said quietly, rising to take his arm. "I want you to meet a friend of Nora's."

Rose walked Berel to Dennis's chair and continued, "Berel, this is Dennis. He's visiting his sister, and we've invited him to dinner. Dennis, I'd like you to meet Berel, a dear friend of our family."

Dennis rose and extended his hand, and Berel reluctantly shook it.

"A friend of the family, Rose?" Berel said. "More like a member, I'd say. I'm Josie's uncle, after all." He looked around the room. "Where is she?"

"Off to bed early tonight. After I fed and bathed her, the poor little thing couldn't keep her eyes open. She was sleeping as soon as I put her down."

Rose invited everybody to the table before there was a chance for further conversation. After the candles were lit and the wine was blessed, the conversation picked up again. Rose asked Dennis where he worked. He told her about his position at a large department store and asked about her shop.

Nora spoke about maintaining herself as a seamstress, and said, "It seems we've all the same problems no matter how big or small the business. Is it the same with you, Berel?"

Berel looked up from his plate. "You don't sound like a Scot, Dennis. Where are you from?"

"From Birmingham. Not Scotland, but not so far away."

"Do you live here now?"

"No, just visiting."

Berel nodded, and went back to eating. Rose noticed that he ate quickly and left the table three times to fill his water glass, though there was a pitcher of water on the table. The longer his silence went on, the more worried Rose became.

At a lull in the conversation during dessert, Berel suddenly asked, "Where were you in the war, Dennis?"

"I served," Dennis said.

"I didn't ask you if you served. I asked where you were while we were fighting the Nazis?"

"I was in London. In a war office."

"Never saw a Nazi, then."

Dennis didn't respond.

"I knew it. You don't look like a man who's ever seen a Nazi. While we were covered in blood and vomit and dying, you were typing all day and stopping for a Guinness every evening."

"My contribution to the war made a difference, just as yours did."

"Don't talk to me about contributions. You don't know a thing about it," Berel snarled. He pushed his chair away from the table, and for a moment, Rose was afraid he meant Dennis harm.

"It's best I leave," he said. "I've a massive headache."

Dennis stayed a bit longer, and then, after making plans with Nora for the next day, he said good night. The two women cleared the table and washed and dried the dishes.

"Berel frightened me tonight. Was it Dennis who set him off?" Nora asked.

"Probably." Rose rinsed the suds off the big roasting pan. "I hadn't properly told Berel who would be here, and any reminder of the war upsets him."

"He can't expect people to make excuses for him. He'll need to get over it if he's to have a normal life."

Rose didn't respond. She couldn't admit that her confidence in Berel's recovery had been shaken by his menacing behavior. Worse yet, she worried that the illusion of family she'd permitted him to create was not contributing to his recovery at all, that it had become nothing more than a dangerous fantasy.

4

AT THE END OF TWELVE WEEKS, THE DAY FINALLY CAME FOR Rose's return to work, and she was eager to see the shop and become part of it again. It isn't that I don't love Josie, she reassured herself, it's that I also love the shop. Each has a separate reservoir of love, and what's given to one doesn't take from the other.

Annie and Henry drove Rose and Josie, along with their two little ones, to Annie's mum's house. After the three children were safely inside and hugged and kissed, the three adults continued on to the shop.

Rose opened the door and stepped inside. It felt like coming home. Comfortable and welcoming. Interesting and inviting. She hoped that customers had the same reaction every time they came in.

It was a busy day. Most of the customers stopped by for a look at Rose, but everybody bought something by way of welcoming her back. Henry was in high spirits as he set off on his first round of visits to the seamstresses and tailors in the area, and when he came back several hours later with book full of orders, Annie and Rose celebrated, too. At closing time, Annie's mum brought the children to the shop. Rose was delighted to see Josie, and it seemed that Josie had saved her biggest smiles of the day for her mother. She launched into a barrage of baby babble.

"It seems she's telling you all about her day," Annie's mum said, "and it was a very good day, indeed. She's an easy baby even though she's a bit loud. She loves watching Annie's little bairns run around, and they love making her laugh."

Rose and Josie were tired after such a big day, and everybody slept well that night.

The routine of their days was set by that first one. Rose thrived on the energy in the shop and watched the business grow with pride. Henry was a valuable addition. Not only did he expand the business, but he also took on much of the bookkeeping so there was no need for Rose to take work home. After a day at the shop, she was free to enjoy Josie in the evening. She and the baby and Nora would eat together before Josie had her bath and everybody fell into bed, sighing audibly before closing their eyes and drifting off to sleep. Rose couldn't imagine a better life. Josie gave her something the shop didn't, and the shop gave her the rest of what she needed.

Only Berel complained that he didn't see Josie enough now that she was away all day long. Annie's mum said he stopped by to see Josie several times a week, but she would not let him take Josie out of the house. At first, he had become furious at her refusal, and his loud voice and angry words had made all the children cry. In fact, Annie's mum admitted, he had frightened her a bit, too. But when he saw how upset the children were, Berel had calmed down immediately and apologized and accepted her explanation that she was paid to be responsible for Josie during the hours the shop was open, and she couldn't pass that responsibility on to anybody else. Now when he visited, he was kind and gentle with all the children, and his earlier outburst seemed like an aberration that should not be held against him.

Rose was glad that Berel had calmed down and apologized to Annie's mum. He had done the same thing when he appeared at her house the morning after his outburst against Dennis. She was eating breakfast when he knocked on the kitchen door.

"I didn't come to intrude on you, Rose, but to ask your forgiveness for my behavior last night," he said. "And please ask Nora to make my apologies to Dennis. I'm sorry for what I said and for the way I acted."

The look on Berel's face had reminded Rose of the day long ago when he had launched an airplane he and her father had

N.R. King

built. The fragile little plane shattered against the trunk of the apple tree, and Berel cried and begged forgiveness for ruining all their hard work. Her father gathered him up and sat with him on the garden bench, hugging him until he stopped crying. "We'll build a better one next week," her father had said.

Berel looked like he had looked that day, and Rose couldn't bear to see him so upset and sad. It's too bad I'm not Papa, she thought. It's too bad I can't hug him and reassure him that everything will be made better next week. "Don't worry, Berel," she said. "I forgive you. But you must see how your anger scares other people."

"It scares me, too," Berel admitted. "But I'm better than I used to be. And it's all due to your kindness. I wouldn't be better at all but for you."

Rose had never wanted to be responsible for his recovery. But how could she jeopardize the progress he had made by refusing to forgive him?

That was how she justified herself to Nora when she relayed the conversation to her.

"I quite agree that he means no harm," Nora said. "But that doesn't mean he won't cause some just the same."

"It's only when he gets upset, that he gets angry."

"But that's what life is, a series of upsets. Things aren't always smooth for any of us."

"Most of us haven't had Berel's experiences. Even Dennis didn't see what Berel saw."

Nora sighed. "We'll all need to be on our guard," she said.

SOMETIMES BEREL CAME BY THE SHOP AT CLOSING TIME when the children were already there and offered Rose and Josie a ride home. Rose accepted because it saved time and trouble for Annie and Henry. Those evenings, Berel stayed for dinner. The four of them would eat together before he left for home and the women moved on with their evening routine.

It's a quiet life, Rose thought, but it's perfect for me. I'm too old for any more adventure than this, and I'm grateful for this much. Though she had to admit to herself that there were moments when she missed Thomas and wondered what her full life would feel like if it brimmed over with his presence.

BEREL WAS AT THE SHOP AT CLOSING TIME ONE DAY IN MAY. He and Rose were enjoying a lighthearted argument about whether or not Josie should have a party to celebrate her year-and-a-half birthday. Berel held that this was an auspicious occasion, and, while not at the level of a yearly birthday, deserved to be marked in some way. Perhaps cake, but no ice cream. Rose maintained that such a celebration would set a precedent and could lead to monthly birthday celebrations, an unthinkable extravagance. And added that Mr. Flay might be the guardian of ritual and tradition, but that she couldn't recall an instance when he had created a new one. Josie was also adding her thoughts in a mix of baby babble and real words all offered up with the cadence and melody of adult conversation. Annie's boys listened in wonder at the torrent of words, and Annie and Henry seemed a little overwhelmed, themselves.

When the door to the shop opened, they all turned in surprise. A customer at this late hour was rare. For a moment, nobody spoke.

Josie looked with wonder at the newcomer, and he looked at her with the same dismay. The rest of the adults could not help looking from one to the other, except for Rose who didn't know where to look.

"Thomas!" Annie said. "What a surprise."

"I've only just arrived from Australia to get my mother and take her back with me now that my dad's passed on," Thomas said. "I wanted to say hello to you," he added, looking at Rose.

Josie walked over to him.

"Who is this?" Thomas asked.

When Rose still said nothing, Annie said, "This is Rose's little girl, Josie."

"A pretty baby," Thomas said. "I'm glad to see her, and to see you, Rose."

Rose had never heard anyone speak in a tone that so belied the content of the words. But what Thomas was really thinking, she could not tell. Nor could she bring herself to answer him.

"I can see you're set to leave for the day. I'll stop back for a proper chat later in the week," Thomas said and left.

"Sorry we didn't get a chance to introduce either of you," Annie said to Henry and Berel. "You don't know Thomas. He was a salesman we knew before he left for Australia. Very nice fellow."

"Oh, I recognize him," Berel said. "It's Steerpike, at last."

After Thomas left, everybody rushed about as though suddenly released from a trance. Berel drove Rose home without another word about Thomas or Josie's half-year birthday. She refused his offer to stay and help with the evening routine, relieved that he didn't realize that Nora was not home to help her. After hurrying Josie through dinner and her bath and into her crib, Rose withdrew to her own room and closed the door.

Steerpike? At first, assigning the people in their lives roles from the strange, gothic book they had both read had been a delightful joke between them. But Rose didn't like Berel's persistence in calling her Countess and referring to Josie as Titus. She liked it even less when the baby started to answer to that name. Annie's mum had refused to answer to Nanny Slagg, especially when she found out that Nanny Slagg was a pitiful, though beloved, midget. And, after she read the book herself, Nora had categorically refused to play the role of Fuschia. Still, Berel maintained the ongoing joke with himself as Mr. Flay, the intensely loyal guardian of the family and keeper of tradition.

Steerpike was the upstart who insinuated himself into the life of the castle and set about to destroy it. He was an enemy of Mr. Flay. Now Berel had assigned that role to Thomas. Thomas, a soft-spoken man, slow moving and well into middle age, seemed an unlikely candidate on the face of it. But Berel was not blinded by appearances. He saw a threat, and he named it.

Rose also recognized Thomas as a threat. The sight of him in the shop had been shocking enough to numb her feelings. But now, though she felt the weight of her shame at having hidden Josie from him, she also recognized her relief that he had found out just the same. This day was always coming, she thought. Just as well that it's here now. And I was happy to see him. The extra beating of this old heart wasn't just shock. It's Thomas who completes the picture. Nobody else. And that's a problem.

Rose heard the front door open and the voices of Nora and Dennis as they came in.

"It seems Rose has gone upstairs. It's a bit early for bed. I hope she's not feeling ill," Nora said. "Would you like a cup of tea?"

"Not tonight. I want to leave you to your thinking. I'll call you tomorrow if that's alright."

"That will be fine. I'll speak to you tomorrow."

Rose heard some murmuring, and then the door opened and closed. Nora came upstairs immediately and knocked softly on her bedroom door.

"Rose," she whispered. "Are you awake?"

"I am. Come right in."

"I hadn't thought the house would be dark and you already in bed. Are you sick? Is something wrong?" Nora asked.

"There's been a bit of excitement, and it wore me out."

"I've had some excitement of my own. Are you well enough to hear about it, or should I wait till the morning?"

"I want to hear it right now," Rose said, sitting up in bed.

Nora pulled the stool from Rose's dressing table to the side of the bed and sat down. "Dennis has proposed. He says that even though we've known each other only a short time, we aren't young anymore, and we've no time to lose. I suppose he means that if there's to be children, we should get to it right away."

"What did you say?"

"I didn't say anything right off. Then I told him I had to think about it. But really there's nothing to think about. I do love him even though it's not the same as with Philip, all that blushing and falling on each other every time we were left alone. And Philip so gallant in his uniform it just about burst my heart to look at him. Neither of us thought for a minute about the danger. We never thought he might not come back.

"This is different, but I think it's just as fine. I don't know why I couldn't say so right away." Nora looked up. "What do you think, Rose?"

"I like Dennis, and I think he'll be a good husband."

"It will change everything, you know. We'll live in Birmingham, for one thing. I never thought I'd leave Scotland and everybody here."

"You have to go where life takes you, Nora. Birmingham isn't exactly the end of the earth. I hear the post runs there now so we'll be able to send letters and pictures. And as soon as they get the lines strung, we'll be able to call on the telephone."

Nora laughed. "You're right. It is a big step, but it's not a giant step." She leaned toward Rose. "I do have another worry, though. How's Berel to find out? I don't want to cause another scene like the one when Dennis came to dinner."

"That's not your worry. I'll take care of it."

"Thank you, Rose. I won't be leaving right away. Dennis will have to go home and prepare his family in Birmingham, and I'll have to go home and prepare my family in Aberdeen. I'll need to be talking to Philip's family, too."

Nora was quiet for a moment. "I'll never be able to repay your kindness to me, and I'll miss you and Josie every day. Will you visit me?"

"You know we will, Nora. And you can come back for visits, too."

Nora smiled. "Now," she said "tell me about the excitement that sent you to bed so early."

Rose hesitated. She didn't want to have this conversation tonight, but Nora, more than anyone else, deserved to know what had happened. She deserved the whole story.

"We had a visitor to the shop today."

"How nice. Who was it?"

"It was a salesman who used to deliver goods to us. He moved to Australia about two years ago."

"It must have been nice to see him again. Is he moving back to Edinburgh?"

"No. He's come to take his mum to Australia with him now that his father's passed on."

"It's lovely that he's come back for her, and nice of him to stop by the shop. But why did that create so much excitement for you?"

"This salesman," Rose hesitated, "he's Josie's father."

"Oh, my."

"Josie marched right up to him, bold as brass, and they looked each other over. She's the spitting image of him, and I have to believe that everybody there saw the resemblance."

"Oh, Rose. What a shock that must have been for you."

"It was a shock for me. And a shock for him, too. He knew nothing about the baby." Rose heard Nora catch her breath. "I've a lot to answer for, Nora."

"I'm sure you had your own good reasons, Rose. Nobody has a right to call you to account."

"Thomas does. He's a lovely man, and I betrayed him. Even as kind as he is, I don't know how he'll react. And there's Berel to worry about. He'll think I owe him something, too. It's a proper mess I've made."

"I'm so sorry, Rose."

"What I've told you hasn't been spoken of yet. It's Thomas who deserves to hear it first."

"Of course."

"Now let's try to sleep." Rose smiled. "We both have big changes coming in our lives, and we need our rest."

The house was quiet. Josie slept peacefully; Nora dozed; and Rose stared at the ceiling.

THE NEXT MORNING, BEREL ARRIVED BRIGHT AND EARLY. Rose and Josie were already in the kitchen when he came through the back door. Rose waited for Berel to make some reference to Thomas, but he made no mention of their encounter at the shop, and neither did she.

"I've come for breakfast, Countess, and to drive you to the shop," he said, taking a spoon from the drawer and sitting in front of Josie's high chair to help her with her porridge.

"Good morning, little Titus. Let me help you get more in your mouth and less on your bib."

Josie was hungry enough to let him help as long as he didn't take her own spoon away. Based on past experience, he knew better than to try.

Later, at the shop, Rose wondered about Berel's good humor. He often had breakfast with them, and it was not unusual for him to help her take Josie to Annie's mum and then drive her to the shop. But the intensity of his high spirits this morning was unsettling.

Friday night dinner that week was just the four of them, as usual. As the evening progressed with no interruption in their routine, Berel grew more relaxed and jovial. Even when Nora said she was meeting Dennis afterwards, Berel's mood didn't change.

After Nora left and Josie was in bed, Rose and Berel sat together in the parlor, she with her knitting and Berel with a book.

"We're like an old married couple, Rose," Berel said. "The two of us in the parlor and the wee one upstairs in her bed."

"Now, Berel, don't mistake our friendship for anything else," Rose said. "It worries me when you talk like that."

"No need to worry, Rose. I'm just saying."

"I've news about Nora."

Berel looked up. "What's that?"

"She and Dennis are planning to marry."

Berel slapped his book closed. "That idiot."

Rose wasn't sure if he meant Dennis or Nora.

"I would have thought Nora had better sense."

"It's not for us to judge," Rose said.

"I imagine we'll see him on Friday nights from now on."

"We are all free to have anybody we want join us, Berel. You know that. But I don't think we'll be seeing them. Nora will be going to Aberdeen to see her family, and then she and Dennis will settle in Birmingham."

Berel sat back in his chair. Rose could see that he was becoming flushed and breathing deeply.

"I hope the news about Nora doesn't upset you, Berel," she said.

"Only that it's hard to believe she would leave you alone in the house after all you've done for her, and it does break up our little family a bit."

"Nora doesn't owe me anything. I'm happy she has a chance for a real family of her own with Dennis, and I wish them well."

"This is a real family, Rose. It's my only family, and it's your only family, too. I thought you would hold it precious."

Another time Rose might have reassured him that their little family would survive, but tonight she had no such assurances to give. "I know this family is a comfort," she said. "But it's not more than a little group of friends who get on well together."

"No!" Berel stood and paced from his chair to the window without looking at her. "I won't have you say that. It's much more. We have saved each other. Dennis is only the beginning. Do you think I don't see that? And I'll not be clueless like Mr. Flay and invite Steerpike in to wreak havoc and destroy us. Flay should have killed him."

"Berel," Rose said, raising her voice. "You can't be wishing harm to another person."

Her loud voice seemed to rouse him, and Berel looked at her intently for a moment before he rushed to the kitchen.

"Do you want a drink of water, Rose?"

"None for me, thank you." Rose could hear the water running.

It was some time before Berel reappeared. His face was red, and his hair was wet. He had straightened his shirt and buttoned his collar. "I've just washed up a bit," he said, and sat down again.

"It will be just the two of us and the baby," Berel said. "We'll be all that's left. But it will be enough. You'll see. It will be enough."

When Rose didn't answer and was quiet for a long time, Berel said, "Goodnight, Rose. I'll see myself out."

Now Rose felt truly alone. She had never wanted to be Berel's only family. How had this happened? There's no one to advise me, she thought. No one to say it will all be fine. Which would be a lie, in any case, because there's no telling if it will be fine or not. What would Papa say? He'd say, "You meant well." It is true that I meant well when I hired Berel to fix the garden. But it's hard to say that I meant well when I left Thomas ignorant of his baby. Rose could imagine her father's look of disappointment, but even though he might sigh, he wouldn't leave it at that. He'd rally his forces, thump the table, and say "No sense crying over spilt milk. Just mean well now." Mean well? For who?

"What kind of question is that?" he'd ask. "For the bairn, of course. For Josie. And for yourself, Rose. Mean well for yourself."

5

EVERY DAY SINCE HIS ARRIVAL, ROSE WAITED FOR THOMAS to reappear. Could it be that he wasn't coming back? Was he so angry? Or so hurt? Maybe it was up to her to contact him. But what would she say?

It was six days before Rose received a little note in the mail. "Dear Rose," it said. "I've needed some time to think, as, perhaps, you have as well. Now I'd like to meet and talk. What do you suggest? Yours, Thomas."

She replied, suggesting that he come to the house the following Wednesday afternoon for tea. Nora offered to go out, but Rose asked simply that she stay upstairs. Without discussing it, neither Rose nor Nora told anyone else about Thomas's visit.

Rose came home on Wednesday afternoon to find that Nora had baked scones and bought a fresh pound of butter and a new jar of fancy marmalade. Thomas arrived right on time carrying a wrapped package that could only be a book. He smiled when Rose answered the door and reached out to kiss her cheek and hug her to him for a long moment. Rose was surprised by his affection. And grateful. Was it this easy to be forgiven?

"This is what I imagined, Rose. And I decided to see if I can make these moments of our reunion just as I imagined them. Thank you for letting me have my way."

Rose had planned to have tea in the parlor, but the formality seemed wrong, now. "I'll set out tea in the kitchen," she said. "It's a bit cozier for just the two of us."

Thomas had never been in the house before, and he took a minute to look around the parlor and the dining room before following her to the kitchen.

"Those are lovely photos you have in the parlor. The girl in the picture on the little table by the couch must be your sister, but who is the boy in the other picture?"

"That boy is Douglas who was our boarder for the five years he was here in medical school."

"So that's Douglas. I often wondered what he looked like. And how he was able to entice your sister to leave Scotland and go with him across the ocean."

"Addy couldn't wait to be on her own."

"So, it wasn't so much finding something new as getting away."

"I think that's probably right."

"You've been left alone in Scotland, Rose."

"Not quite alone," Rose said, blushing.

"Not quite alone," Thomas repeated and sat at the table.

Rose poured their tea and set out the scones and butter and jam.

Thomas poured a drop of milk in his cup and helped himself to a scone. "You didn't bake these. I remember your scones too well to think you made these."

"Nora, the lady who also lives here, made them."

"They're very good, but they're not like I remember yours."

Rose started to answer, but Thomas interrupted her. "Let me continue my little fantasy. I went over and over it in my mind every day of the voyage here. How I would see you and hug you. And then I would tell you about Australia."

Rose nodded, and he went on.

"Even though it's busy and there's a surprise every day, Australia is a peaceful place. My brother-in-law's business is doing well, and I enjoy the work. I own a house and a car. It's been a good two years." Thomas sipped his tea and smiled at Rose. "Except for missing you.

"I didn't need to come back for my mother. We have a cousin who is also emigrating, and she could have brought my mother over with her. But I offered to get Mum because I hoped to convince you to return with me. So, you see, I came with a plan, and since I'm not a subtle man, I've told you my plan straight off." Thomas laughed and shook his head.

"I never dared ask you to come with me before. I didn't know what I would find there. I didn't know if I would stay. And I couldn't bear hearing you say that you wouldn't join me. So I held my tongue and said nothing."

"Why didn't you write to me once you were there? Or let me know that you were coming back to Scotland?"

"I'm sorrier for that than you can know. When I got to Australia, I knew that it had been a mistake to come without you. But I was no better at telling you that by letter than I had been at pleading my case in person. Week after week and then month after month, I put off writing, until it seemed too late." Thomas put down his teacup. "I'm a cowardly person, Rose. There's the truth of it. I couldn't bring myself to put the question until I was sure of the answer. I hope it's not too late now that the situation is more complicated." He hesitated a minute before continuing. "Forgive me, but I need to ask. The little one. She's mine, isn't she?"

Rose nodded. "She is." And waited for the recriminations to begin.

"I never thought that I would have a family," Thomas said. "I was hoping for you as a wife, but now to think that I also have a child is more happiness than I dared to wish for."

"Do you want to talk about Josie?"

"I do, but not now. Now let's go step-by-step. That's what I imagined. Let's get to know each other again, in the open this time. Let's laugh together like we used to, and take pleasure in each other's company like we used to, and let me tell you more about life in Australia. It's six months until I sail. Plenty of time to enjoy spring and summer here and get to Sydney in time for spring and summer there."

Before he left, Thomas gave Rose the package he had with him, a book as she had guessed. "My sister chose it for you.

She said it's a grand story, and by a Brit who just emigrated to Australia, himself. She hopes you like it."

After they planned a stroll during Rose's lunch break the next day, Thomas left.

ROSE AND THOMAS WALKED TOGETHER THREE OR FOUR times a week for the next three weeks. They got to know each other again, laughed together, and took pleasure in each other's company, just as Thomas had planned. And, just as he had planned, Thomas told her about Australia.

As they sat on a bench in the Princes Street Gardens, he told her about Australia's strange animals and friendly people and assured her that immigrants were welcome and made to feel at home. Looking across the gardens to the castle in the distance, Thomas described his little house in Bondi. "I live not far from Sydney on the most beautiful beach in the world," he said. "There's a walk along the cliff top from Bondi to Coogee where you'll see sights you've never seen before. It's more lovely than you can imagine."

They visited museums and climbed monuments, and talked about the sights in Sydney. "We've the biggest harbor in the world," Thomas said, "with the longest bridge ever built going right across it. You can see it from everywhere. And every Sunday we can go to a great open meadow called the Domain where people stand on soap boxes and carry on about whatever's on their minds. We'll pack a picnic lunch and go to listen. Or maybe we'll bring a box to stand on and tell the crowd a thing or two, ourselves."

They browsed at Jenner's, critiquing the merchandise and the demeanor of the salesladies. "Australia is like nowhere else on earth," Thomas told her. "It's a place to be happy."

N.R. King

Rose believed him, and with that thought, she became alarmed. He's winning me over, she thought. I'm actually imagining what it would be like to return with him.

Australia might seem like an exciting possibility when she was with Thomas, but as soon as she returned to the shop, Rose doubted she could ever leave Scotland. Too much would be left behind.

ROSE HAD TOLD ANNIE THAT THOMAS WAS JOSIE'S FATHER, but that she wasn't ready, yet, to tell Berel or make the news public. Annie understood and had not spoken of it, even to Henry. The same discretion could not be expected of Mrs. Carter, who happened to be in the shop one afternoon when Thomas came by for Rose. She scrutinized and appraised him from every angle while fingering merchandise and trying on gloves. As soon as he left with Rose, she turned on Annie.

"Who is that?" she demanded.

"That fellow was a salesman here before he emigrated to Australia."

"Why is Rose going about with him?"

"I wouldn't say they are going about. They're friends."

"I'd say it's more than that. I saw the baby last week when your mum had all the children at the park. Now that I've had a good look at this salesman, I wouldn't be surprised if he was involved," Mrs. Carter said, looking closely at Annie for any telltale reaction.

Annie, practiced in the ways of a close-knit, talkative community, showed no reaction at all.

"Just as I thought," Mrs. Carter sniffed, practiced in the ways of noncommittal salesladies.

"Mrs. Carter has you pegged," Rose told Thomas as they walked up the block. "It won't take long for the word to get out."

Thomas nodded.

"I know it's long past time for me to talk, Thomas, but I don't know what to say. I feel like a thief, and now that you're here again, I can't understand how I could do such a thing. I was terribly selfish, and I'm sorry." Rose began to cry and fumbled in her bag for a tissue.

"Take my arm, Rose," Thomas said, handing her his handkerchief. "I'm glad you've spoken so that now I can say I forgive you. I do forgive you, Rose, with my whole heart."

Rose began to cry in earnest, and Thomas found them a bench to sit on. He drew her close and sat with his arm around her as she calmed herself. She rested her head on his chest.

"Thank you, Thomas. I'm grateful to be forgiven."

"And I'm grateful we have another chance. But we won't have that chance if we look back. From this moment, we need to look only forward."

"It's just that I didn't see any solution then. I didn't want to leave my shop, and you didn't want to stay in Scotland. I can't say that I see a solution even now."

"It's too soon for solutions. Let's just think about today and tomorrow. I want to meet Josie and spend time being her dad. I wrote my sister in Australia about her, and she's sent Josie a gift that I want to give her."

Rose realized that Thomas had only been waiting for her to speak about Josie before he proposed a change in their agreement. She appreciated his patience and knew that his requests were not unreasonable. But she was reluctant just the same. I'm still selfish, she thought. I don't want to share her with anybody else, especially someone who has a fair claim on her.

Thomas noticed Rose's hesitation. "Don't worry, Rose. It's your happiness I want. You are the reason I came back to Scotland. And these weeks with you have shown me how right I was to come back. I want to return to Sydney with you and with Josie." Thomas laughed. "But I don't plan to take you in chains like the first colonists. I think it would be a grand adventure for the both of us, and a wonderful place for Josie to grow up. I was too timid to ask you to take that risk before, but now that I know it would be a good decision, I'll not make that mistake again."

"What about the shop?"

"Annie and Henry would love to have the shop and keep it going just as it is. And I would help you open another like it in Australia."

"It was my father's shop."

"And wouldn't he be proud to see you opening a new shop in a foreign land? Just like he did."

Rose hadn't thought of that before, and she wondered if Thomas was right.

"And Josie would have a mum and a dad." Thomas paused. "But I don't want you to agree because you think it's your duty. You've done your duty all your life, Rose…with just a wee bit of mischief now and again," he added smiling at her before becoming serious again. "Now I want you to think about what would make you happy, and I hope that means coming to Australia with me."

Rose sighed. Thomas might be kind and patient, she thought, but he's also determined. Is he winning me over or wearing me down?

As soon as she came back to the shop, Rose told Annie that she and Thomas had talked about Josie, and there was no more need for secrecy.

"It's well you're ready to share the news because I'm quite sure the news is making the rounds."

"Mrs. Carter."

"Quite right."

The speed with which Mrs. Carter's surmise became a certitude and traveled through the community was unprecedented. Furtive whispers became a muffled roar and burst forth in ravenous shrieks of dismay. "He's back? Shows up on her doorstep one day, just like that? The scoundrel!"

The ladies wanted to know his name and who his people were and where they were from. They thought it appropriate that he was, as Mrs. Carter described him, older. At least he's not some young bounder. Did he plan to take Rose and the baby back to Australia? Or would he stay here and do his duty by her like a gentleman? Or, horrors, would he steal Josie and take her off to that god-forsaken place on the other side of the world? If we ever catch him out and about by himself, they agreed, he'll get an earful.

The shop became crowded with ladies watching Rose for clues and hoping for a peek at Thomas. Fortunately, they usually bought something to justify their visits and business was good. But Rose had to tell Thomas to stay away for the time being.

Annie finally suggested that Rose take a little holiday from the shop. "I can manage here, and Josie can still go to my mum. That way, it might be easier for you to sort things out. At least you won't have an audience," she added.

Rose decided to take two weeks at home. Henry and Annie stopped by every morning to take Josie to Annie's mum for the day and leave a folder of paperwork for Rose to sign. After the children had been dropped off and Annie was at the shop, Henry came back to pick up the paperwork and chat briefly with Rose about his plans for the day. The business was growing, and he was eager to expand to outlying districts.

Thomas came by in the midmorning and stayed for lunch. Rose looked forward to his daily visits. It was gratifying to see how much he enjoyed her company, and she realized that she enjoyed his in equal measure. There was also a quickening in her body that she recognized, and it amused her to think that she was not so elderly, after all.

When Thomas reached for her one afternoon, she returned his embrace. His hunger for her ignited Rose's own desire, and she felt fortunate that Nora was in Aberdeen and they had the house to themselves.

That afternoon, they went together to collect Josie from Annie's mum. This was the second time Josie had seen Thomas, and she smiled broadly when he came into the house. Rose introduced Thomas to Annie's mum and then turned to Josie.

"Josie, this is your dad," she said.

"Hi, Da," Josie said as if it was the most natural thing in the world to be introduced to your father one sunny afternoon when you are already more than one-and-a-half years old. And maybe she thought it was. Maybe she thought that's just how Jeffrey and Ian had met their father, her Uncle Henry. Uncles, you meet right away, but Da doesn't come around until later.

Annie's little boys were much more impressed. "Like our Da, only Josie's?" Ian asked his grandmother.

"Quite right," she said.

"Good," Ian said. "Now she has one of her own. She'll see it's much nicer than only having uncles."

Thomas stayed for dinner and helped with Josie's bath and bed. She was pleased with the stuffed kangaroo her Aunt Lydia had sent her from Australia and was persuaded not to take it in her bath only when Rose suggested sitting it on the toilet seat to watch. After Josie was tucked in for the night, Rose and Thomas sat together in the parlor.

"She's a lovely little girl, Rose. I'm proud she's mine and proud you are her mother."

"Thank you, Thomas. I have to say that I'm proud you are her father. The two of you get along like you've known each other all her life." Rose paused and shook her head. "I wish you had."

"Remember, Rose, we aren't looking back. I can't have you sad. That's not like you."

"Nothing about this was like me. I didn't understand myself at all, and then I pretended it hadn't happened. I pretended this moment would never come."

"I'm glad it has, and I don't plan on spending it regretting what's past. You're a great mum, and I plan on being a great dad. All I'm asking is that you give me the chance to make you happy. It isn't only Josie I love, you know."

Rose smiled at him. "This time with you is making me happy, Thomas. I never let myself realize it before, but now I see how much I missed you."

When Thomas got up to leave, Rose followed him to the front door. They were saying good night when they heard the back door open and a male voice call from the kitchen, "Rose, are you in the parlor? Sorry it's so late. I started a new garden and just washed up. I've put your mower back in the shed, and I've something to give you."

"Who is that?" Thomas asked, just as Berel appeared and asked, "What's he doing here?"

"Berel, this is Thomas. He's visiting."

"Josie's father, right? My mother is full of the news. Couldn't wait to tell me. Not that I didn't already know. Were you planning to mention it, Rose?"

"I've only just told Josie, and, of course, I was going to tell you."

"Too bad my mum beat you to it."

Berel turned to Thomas. "The dad. Where were you when Josie was born? Are you the one who brought Rose flowers in the hospital? Did you paint Josie's room?" Berel's face grew red, and he tugged at his shirt. "You've been some dad, so far, and you'll not show up unannounced and steal her now. I won't let you."

"Please, Berel," Rose said. "No need to get upset."

"Not like you to lie, Rose."

"You've no right to raise your voice to Rose," Thomas said to Berel. And then to Rose, quietly added, "I don't think I'll leave just yet."

"No. Leave," Berel shouted. "That's what you're good at. Running away. It would be a sight better if you had stayed away." He turned to go upstairs.

"Where are you going?" Rose asked.

"Upstairs to give Josie a good night kiss."

"She's already asleep, Berel."

"I'll just give her a good night kiss."

"She's sleeping, Berel. You'll wake her."

Berel began to pound on the bannister as he shouted into Rose's face. "Are you keeping her from me? You've never done that before."

"You aren't yourself, Berel. This isn't a good time for you to visit."

"Are you telling me to leave, Rose?"

"I think it's best."

"Banished, am I? Banished? Just like Flay? And what's to become of our little family? Who will protect it, if I don't?" Berel banged his fist on the bannister one more time and turned back to the kitchen. "I've left you a book on the table, Countess. It's all in there. Read it and come to your senses." He walked through the kitchen and slammed the back door as he left.

Thomas and Rose stood in silence at the front door.

"I'm sorry Berel believes you knew I was pregnant when you left," she said. "And I'm ashamed that I didn't defend you to him." She couldn't bring herself to admit how grateful she was that Thomas hadn't told Berel the truth.

"He wouldn't have listened, and it doesn't matter what he thinks. We're not going to explain ourselves to anybody." Thomas hugged her and smoothed her hair. "But what does he mean by 'our little family'? He can't believe that Josie is his child."

Rose told Thomas about the young man Berel had been before the war, about his relationship with her father when he was a little boy, and about hiring him as her gardener. She also related the story of his offer to be Josie's father and described his attachment to Josie and to her.

"I know you feel sorry for him," Thomas said, "but you've let him live with his illusions long enough. I don't think he should come here anymore. And I don't think you should let him near Josie."

"He would never hurt Josie, and I know he'll be sorry for the scene he made tonight."

"Don't fool yourself, Rose. We had a man like Berel working for us in Sydney. All tense and making outbursts. We put up with it until one day somebody mistook his jacket for their own and he broke the windshield of the fellow's car calling him a thief and threatening to kill him." Thomas took her hand. "Look at me Rose. It's lovely that you are so ready to see the best in others, but it's leading you astray here. Berel is dangerous."

After Thomas left, Rose went into the kitchen. On the table was a package wrapped in bright green paper and tied with a ribbon. Rose took it upstairs, sat on her bed, and carefully untied the ribbon and pulled away the paper. *Gormenghast*. The sequel to *Titus Groan*.

The book Thomas had given her, *A Town Like Alice*, was already on her nightstand. The cover showed a colorful vista of red-roofed houses with green hills in the distance. Rose put the book from Berel next to it and looked at its cover. A storm of flames burst into the sky over a crumbling castle. There were no colors but black and dusty white.

6

BEREL CONTINUED TO CARE FOR THE GARDEN, BUT HE NO longer came to the shop or into the house. Rose didn't go outside when he was in the backyard. She had nothing to say that would reassure him and was afraid of precipitating another scene. Annie's mum reported that he came by every few days and spent a little while playing with Josie or helping with her lunch. He was always quiet and respectful and didn't try to take Josie out of the house. Rose knew she had to take Thomas's warning seriously, but she couldn't help hoping that Berel's outburst would fade from everyone's memory and all would be well.

It's just a momentary setback, she told herself. There's been two or three before, but they've never undone his recovery. He needs sympathy, not punishment, friends, not accusers. I can't overlook how hard he's worked, how far he's come. What would Papa say if I abandoned him now?

Thomas visited every day and stayed for dinner every evening. He and Josie got on famously, and Nora also enjoyed his company.

"He's easy to be with, but he's not boring," she said. "Underneath his quiet manner is a man who loves adventure. I can see why you like him."

And Rose did like him. She more than liked him. She could remember a time when her life seemed complete and she savored the peace and calm of it. But now, when she compared her life in Edinburgh with the possibility of a life in Sydney, she began to feel as adventuresome as Thomas. Almost.

"What if I come to Australia with you for a visit?" she asked him one night after dinner.

"It's a long way for a visit, but I suppose that would be alright."

"What if I come with you, and it doesn't work out?"

"I think we'll need to be quite sure it will work out before we leave Scotland."

"What if I go to Australia, and I want to come back to Edinburgh."

"Then you'll come back, of course. I want you to be my wife, not my prisoner."

"What if I don't want to come to Australia at all? Would you go back without me?"

"I don't think I could live there without you, and I don't think I could give up Josie. So I suppose I would stay here. But I think the three of us will be happiest if we are together in Sydney. I think you will be very happy there."

It came as a surprise to Rose that Thomas would stay in Scotland for her.

"Remember the war, Rose? Remember the feeling of being part of something big, something important?"

Rose nodded. She did remember how every day had tingled with possibility. How every effort was celebrated and every emotion capitalized.

"Australia is like that without the killing and the danger. Every morning there's a new reason to jump out of bed. Every day there's something new to build and somebody new to meet. My money will keep us, and we'll open a shop for you. Another J. Kaminsky, Draper, on the other side of the world. Wouldn't you like that?"

Rose knew she would, but she couldn't quite say so yet. "Maybe I'm a bit old for this much adventure."

Thomas laughed. "You're never too old for an adventure. Not you. Two years ago, we had an adventure, and now we can have another. I loved you then, and I love you now. We are a good partnership, Rose."

Sweet, ardent Thomas, Rose thought. You're right. But she didn't say anything.

Rose did, however, read the book that Thomas had given her, and realized that his sister had chosen the perfect gift to make his case. The main character, Jean, was a woman Rose could understand, a woman she might like to be identified with. Rose knew that the war had not been nearly so harrowing for her as it was for Jean, but she liked to think she shared Jean's determination and instinct to survive. When Joe described Australia to Jean, Rose could hear the same love of the country she heard when Thomas talked to her about Sydney. When Jean traveled to Australia to look for Joe, Rose admired her resolve, and wished she had had the fortitude to pack up Josie and go searching for Thomas. When Joe went to England to look for Jean, Rose worried they would never find each other.

The happy ending pleased her. Joe gave Jean a family, a business, and a life filled with adventure and love. Just what Thomas offered her. Why hesitate? This chance won't come again, she told herself. Don't miss it now. Isn't that what Papa would say? Rose could imagine how his eyes would light up at the thought of a daughter with a family and another shop with his name on it in a place he never imagined.

Another week went by, filled with Thomas's comforting presence or thoughts of Thomas when he wasn't there. Until, finally, Rose knew she needed no more time, though it made her a little dizzy when she envisioned the step she was about to take.

At dinner one night when Nora was out, Rose took Thomas's hand and said, "I've decided to come with you, Thomas. It's what I want to do."

"Rose, my wonderful Rose," Thomas said, grinning at her. "I couldn't be happier."

Josie stared at them while they kissed and then said, "Me, too."

"There's something else we need to take care of," Thomas said.

"I know," Rose answered. "I hope you agree we need no fanfare."

"Quite right. Joyous in a quiet way."

"And we'll be making no announcement, so by the time people realize, it will be old news."

"Right again."

"And no guests but close friends and family."

"We'll need to agree on the guest list, Rose."

"That will be our first negotiation," she said, laughing.

"You're a determined man, Thomas, but know that I'm a determined woman."

"One of the best things about you," Thomas said.

That evening Rose knocked on Nora's bedroom door.

"Come right in," Nora said.

"Sorry to interrupt you," Rose said when she saw Nora propped up in bed writing a letter.

"You're no interruption, Rose. I'm glad to see you."

"It's my turn for news," Rose began. "I've decided to go to Australia with Thomas." As she said it for the first time aloud, Rose couldn't believe her ears. Had she really decided to do such a thing? It seemed momentous when she said it. More than anyone should be able to fit into one sentence.

"What a grand adventure, Rose," Nora said.

"I hope adventures aren't overrated."

"Are you feeling uncertain?"

Rose thought for a minute. "Not uncertain, just overwhelmed at the thought of such a big change and when I think about all that will need to be done if I'm to sail with Thomas in just a few months."

THOMAS WENT TO SEE THE RABBI AND TOOK CARE OF THE necessary applications, and Nora began a new dress for Rose. For the moment, nobody else was told. Thomas and Rose set to work on the guest list: Thomas's mother, Nora and Dennis, Annie and Henry and Annie's mum, which meant that Ian and Jeffrey and Josie would be cared for by a neighbor. Rose thought there was no point in inviting her sister since she was sure not to come. So far, the list had been easy to agree on. It was when they came to the question of Berel that problems arose.

"I don't want him there," Thomas said. "He doesn't wish us well, and this won't be a celebration for him. I will be worried about his reaction every minute he's in the house."

"He's Josie's uncle," Rose began.

"He's not Josie's uncle, and that little fiction is one of the reasons he worries me."

"He needed that fiction. That fiction helped him, and he helped us. He's been a good friend."

"He didn't help you. You helped him. It was wonderful of you, and I admire you. But you must admit that he hasn't recovered. It's sad that the war affected him so badly, but you aren't a miracle worker, Rose, and you don't owe him more than you've already done. The time has come to show him that he's on his own."

Part of Rose knew that Thomas was right. But what would her father think if the boy he had loved was abandoned without a word? Didn't Berel deserve a chance to make amends and share her happiness? "He can't be left out. That would be cruel, and I won't do it," Rose said.

The negotiations stopped there for the day.

When talks resumed the next day, both Rose and Thomas had softened their stances. Each agreed that the position of the other had some merit.

"My only concern is for Berel," Rose said. "I don't need him there, but I think he needs to be there."

"My concern is for all of us, and I think he has too little control of himself to be included. He's put himself in a privileged position in your life. I don't blame you for that, but I do wish you had been more careful."

"You think I misled him."

"No, I think you permitted him to mislead himself, and you did it only for the best of reasons. You're a wonderful woman, Rose. Sometimes, too wonderful for your own good."

Nonetheless, Rose continued to insist that Berel be on the guest list, and Thomas continued to insist that he was unwelcome.

By the third day, their positions remained unchanged, and neither had new arguments to put forth.

"We're not doing well at persuading each other," Thomas said wearily. "I hope this isn't an indication of how exhausting a wife you're going to be."

Rose laughed and hugged him. "You must admit that we are well matched," she said. "Do you agree that it's time to compromise?"

"So long as the compromise doesn't begin with my surrender," Thomas said.

At last, it was agreed that Rose would talk to Berel in a public space or in the house if Nora was home. She would tell him that she planned to marry Thomas and that she and Josie would be emigrating to Australia in a few months. She could say that Berel had been wonderful to them and that they would write him letters, but she also had to emphasize that she loved Thomas and was excited about her new life in Australia. It was further agreed that they wouldn't tell anybody else about their plans until Berel was told. After Rose shared his reactions with Thomas, they would decide if he took the news calmly enough to be included on the wedding guest list.

FOR SEVERAL DAYS ROSE WATCHED FOR BEREL. WHILE SHE waited, she read the book he had given her and became increasingly concerned about him the more she read and the longer it took for him to appear.

In the new volume, the Countess banishes Flay from the castle. Now Rose understood why Berel had been so upset the night she asked him to leave and why he hadn't returned. Flay lives as a wild man in the woods and watches over the castle, vowing to kill Steerpike before Steerpike destroys the family. Rose was alarmed. How far had Berel sunk into this fantasy?

Early the next morning, Rose went out to the shed where Berel kept his tools to leave a note asking him to come into the kitchen for tea and a chat the next day. She thought the shed would be closed and locked, but, instead, she found the door open and Berel inside, sleeping on a mound of blankets.

"Berel," she said. "Wake up and come in the house."

Berel sat up, fully awake instantly. "Rose, you've come for me. I knew you would."

Rose was shocked at how dirty he was. His hands and face were caked with grime and his clothing was soiled and torn. "You can't be sleeping in the shed. This isn't healthy, Berel."

Berel followed her inside and washed up in the downstairs bathroom while she made tea and toast. He ate so quickly that Rose also fixed him a bowl of porridge and some eggs.

"You seem quite famished, Berel," she said. "When did you eat last?"

"It's been a day or two."

"Have you been working?"

"No. I've had to watch the house, Rose. We are all in danger."

"Does this have to do with the book you gave me?"

"Yes. I knew you would see it all in the book. Steerpike is here and plans to destroy us. He wants to kill me. I've had to become a man of the woods, like Flay. The Countess saw the danger, so you must see it, too. Our Titus is too young to understand, too little to kill him. It's up to me to save us."

Rose looked as him in despair. "Berel," she said quietly, "I am not the Countess and you are not Flay and Thomas does not want to kill you. This is not the book."

Berel pushed his plate away, and looked at her.

"Berel, do you understand? Thomas does not want to kill you or anybody else."

Berel nodded. "I've not been sleeping well. Some nights not at all. I'm losing track of things, and I can't let that happen. It's like the war, Rose. I can't go back there."

"That was a terrible time, but it's over. You take care of gardens now and make beautiful things grow."

Berel smiled. "I knew you would understand. Nobody else understands, but you always do. I was all alone until you understood. Thanks for breakfast. I do feel better."

Rose didn't know what to say next. The wedding would be soon, and Berel needed to know about it. This might not be the right time to say something, but she didn't know if she would get a better chance.

"I'm glad you're feeling better because I need to tell you about some changes in our lives, Berel."

Berel looked at her intently. "He's won. Are you going to tell me he's won?"

"Thomas and I are…"

"Don't say it. I don't want to hear the words. He's ripping my family apart. Now there's nobody. There'll never be anybody. He might as well kill me. I wish he would kill me."

Berel leapt out of his chair and smashed his fist on the table, spilling the rest of his tea and sending his plate to the floor.

"I thought you understood, but you don't," he shouted. "Everything will be empty again. Everything will be cold."

Rose could hear Nora running down the stairs. Berel heard the footsteps, too, and, as Nora rushed into the kitchen, he screamed and pushed her away so roughly that she fell onto the shards of the plate. Berel stared at her crawling away from him and reached down to touch the growing pool of blood.

"It's here, Rose," he yelled. "Do you see it? The war. It found me here. I'll never get away." Berel held out his bloody hands before wiping them on his shirt. "There's no safe place."

Rose was too stunned to react before Berel raced through the dining room. She heard the glass in the breakfront shatter and more things crash to the floor in the parlor. Finally, she heard the front door slam shut.

The silence in the house was too quiet. Where had Berel gone? Where was Nora? Rose found her sitting on the edge of the bathtub, crying.

"Are you badly hurt?"

Nora lifted the edge of her skirt and held out her hand. There were many cuts, but none seemed serious enough to warrant a trip to the hospital. Rose cleaned and bandaged them quickly.

"You'll have a bruise where you came down." she said. "I'm so sorry you were hurt."

"I've never seen a man in a rage before. It's the most frightened I've ever been."

"I was frightened, too, Nora."

"We should call the police, Rose."

"It wouldn't do Berel any good to be locked up."

"But he's not in his right mind. He might attack someone else."

Just what Thomas would say, Rose thought.

When Nora saw Rose hesitate, she said, "I'll call the constable and ask him to come by here, and I'll call Annie's mum in case Berel tries to see Josie."

Rose nodded. Nora was right, those phone calls had to be made. But Berel needs help from someone who sees him as more than a dangerous man. More than the person he is right now. "While you make the phone calls, I'll go to see Berel's mother," Rose said. "Can I leave you alone in the house?"

"Be careful, Rose. There's no telling where Berel ran off to."

ROSE DIDN'T SEE BEREL ON HER WAY TO HIS HOUSE. SHE knocked on the door and waited quite a while before using the big metal knocker to make a louder sound. At last, Mrs. Gerstein opened the front door. Rose saw that she had been crying.

"Come in," she said and led the way to the parlor. "Please sit down while I get us some tea."

"No need," Rose said.

"I insist," Mrs. Gerstein said and disappeared into the kitchen.

Moments later they were sipping tea. She must have had the kettle already hot, Rose thought. "I just want a minute to talk to you about Berel."

"I thought so," Mrs. Gerstein said.

"Do you know where he is now?" Rose asked.

"He's upstairs, asleep."

Rose was surprised and relieved that Berel hadn't suffered any harm or done further damage.

"Can you tell me what happened to him?" Mrs. Gerstein asked. "Why did he come home in the middle of the morning, with blood on his hands and his shirt after not being home at all for days?"

"He was at my house earlier, and I'm afraid there was a bit of a scene. I'm relieved he's safe."

"Henry Epsin brought Berel home in his car. As soon as I opened the door, Berel came flying in, babbling about danger and blood and Nazis. He said they were trying to kill him." Mrs. Gerstein shook her head. "I hadn't seen him like that for years."

She took her handkerchief from the pocket of her apron and wiped her eyes. "Henry didn't know what had happened. Do you know whose blood it was? Did he hurt somebody?"

"Berel was at my house, and Nora got cut on pieces of a plate that broke. It was an accident. Berel didn't mean to hurt her. He ran out before we could tell him that she's not badly cut."

Mrs. Gerstein nodded. "Good. I was afraid he had attacked somebody. He's never done that before."

"He didn't attack anybody or mean anybody harm."

"I didn't know what to do with him all bloody and carrying on. I called the doctor, and Henry stayed until Dr. Fields got here. Came right away, he did. The younger one who's a bit more up to date. Berel let the two men clean him off so Dr. Fields could see if he was injured. Then the doctor gave Berel something to drink, and now he'll sleep for a long while." Mrs. Gerstein sighed and wiped her eyes.

"Dr. Fields said he'll be back tonight to talk about what we should do next. He said that Berel isn't the only one to come back different from the war, and that he'll have to go to hospital for a time. Some men can't be helped, he told me, but Berel is good with plants and he has a business. 'Don't you worry,' he said. 'We can help men who've been strong enough to help themselves.' That's what he said."

"I'm so sorry this happened," Rose said.

"We're all of us sorry."

"I never meant Berel any harm."

"Sometimes I wish he had never met you or worked in your garden. Sometimes I would like to hate you, Rose, and blame everything on you. But I know this isn't your fault. I believe that what you did was done with a good heart."

Mrs. Gerstein started to cry again, and Rose reached for her own handkerchief.

"I'm his own mother, and I couldn't help him. None of us knew how to help Berel."

The two women sat quietly together for a time. Finally, Rose shared the news of her departure for Australia, and Berel's mother wished her well. She said that Rose could write to her and she would send Rose news of Berel and share Rose's news with him if the doctors thought it wise.

———————

By the time Rose came home, the kitchen had been cleaned, and Thomas was standing at the window. Rose began to cry when she saw him.

"Shhhh," he said, holding her close. "I'm here. You're not alone, anymore. I'll always be here to help you." He smoothed Rose's hair away from her face and helped her to a chair before sitting down, himself.

"The constable was here when I arrived, and Nora told us both what happened," he said. "Then Henry came by and told us the rest. He said he had come back for the paperwork he'd left earlier and just parked his car when he saw Berel burst out of the house covered in blood. It had been quite a while since he had seen anybody in that state—not since the war—and he reacted just as the men did then. He grabbed Berel and held him. Henry's a big man so even though Berel struggled, he couldn't escape. And while he held Berel, Henry sang, soft and slow. 'By yon bonnie bank and by yon bonnie braes where the sun shines bright on Loch Lomond.' By the time he got to 'Ye'll take the high road and I'll take the low road,' Berel had relaxed. He let Henry put him in the car and take him to his mother. After the constable heard the whole story, and Nora assured him that she didn't want Berel to be arrested, it was agreed that there was no need to involve the police."

Thomas reached across the table and took Rose's hand. "It's been a trying morning, Rose. Nora said you went to see Berel's mother. You should have waited for me to go with you."

"No. I needed to go by myself. It was a conversation for just the two of us."

"I hope she wasn't unkind."

"No, she wasn't. She was just sad, and so was I." Rose looked up at Thomas. "How could everything have gone so wrong? Now it seems cruel to have shared our lives with Berel."

"It wasn't cruel, Rose. You didn't see this day coming, and you never intended to hurt him."

Thomas and Rose washed the blood stains off the candlestick Berel had thrown through the breakfront and cleaned up the glass on the dining room floor.

"This was the first piece of real furniture my parents bought after they came to this country," Rose said. "All they had in the house were the beds, the kitchen table, and four chairs when they bought this big, beautiful breakfront. My mother said they needed a fitting place for my father's kiddush cup, and for a long time, it was the only thing on the shelves."

"We'll have it repaired," Thomas said, "and we'll take it with us. And anything else you would like to have from Scotland."

The damage in the parlor was less easily dealt with. Berel had broken all the picture frames, and the photographs of Rose's family had been ripped. Rose couldn't bear to discard them, so the paper fragments were sealed in an envelope to be taken to Australia.

7

It was a small wedding. They gathered in the rabbi's study, Rose and Thomas, his mother, Nora and Dennis, Annie and Henry, and Annie's mum.

Thomas moved into Rose's house, and the neighbors saw him leaving every morning to take her to the shop and Josie to Annie's mum. They also noticed the wedding band on her finger, and they approved. The ladies at the shop saw the band, too. "Very pretty," they clucked. "Lovely that he's made her an honest woman, and very kind of her to let him make amends. And they're off to Australia in just a month or two. Imagine that. Never thought that Rose would leave her father's shop, but Annie says she's to open one just like it in Australia. And there will be letters from Australia for us to read when we stop by the original J. Kaminsky, Draper, to see Annie and pick up a new pair of gloves or some ribbon.

"It's a shame about poor Berel, of course. Couldn't bear to see Rose leave Scotland, it seems, but that's not her fault. And if Frieda bears her no ill will, neither do we. We're as magnanimous as she is. More, really.

8

Rose never went back to Scotland. Neither did Thomas or Josie. The second J. Kaminsky, Draper did well, and Rose grew old looking after the shop and Thomas and being looked after by Thomas, in return. Eventually, the original J. Kamisky, Draper was inherited by Ian and grew into a much bigger store, and the second J. Kaminsky, Draper was inherited by Josie who married Ian's brother, Jeffrey, when he came on holiday one summer. He claimed to remember her from their early childhood when they were both cared for by his grandmother. He said no other girl could please him after knowing Josie, even though she'd been a toddler at the time.

"Absurd," the daughters of the original Kaminsky's customers agreed. "If it hadn't really happened, we never would have believed it. But it does rather tickle the fancy to have Rose's stores, so far apart, looked after by brothers."

NORA AND DENNIS LIVED OUT THEIR LIVES IN BIRMINGHAM and had three sons in their first five years of marriage. All the boys grew tall and sturdy like their father. Even though Nora thought Dennis a bit too devoted to his mother, she loved him, still.

BEREL RETURNED TO EDINBURGH BUT STAYED JUST TWO weeks with his mother before he returned to the hospital. Eventually, he was considered well enough to move into a small cabin on the grounds and assume responsibility for tending the gardens. He planted new flower beds in front of the buildings and a vegetable garden in the back.

Berel lived with a small, old dog who had found her way to his doorstep. He called her Trixie and enticed her to stay with scraps from his table. She slept on the grass or in a corner of the vegetable garden while he went through his day and curled up at his feet in the evening. Berel knew he had to wake up every morning to feed her. And because he had to wake up every morning, he got through every night.

ACKNOWLEDGMENTS

MY GRATITUDE TO ALL THOSE WHO ENCOURAGED ME TO write. I have been blessed with gifted and supportive writing teachers, including: Margaret Osborne, my first writing teacher, who showed me what it meant to be a writer; Tim Johnston, who nurtures and inspires every student; Bill Black, whose generous mentoring guided this book through its final draft; Faye Moskowitz, whose well of human kindness never runs dry; Michelle Brafman, who said "Go for it," when that was just what I needed to hear; and Jean Graubart, whose goodwill and hard work never fail to inspire.

Special thanks to Susan Helsel, Elaine Logan, Sarah Arno, Kathy Wouk, Gloria Neubert, and the participants in workshops at Johns Hopkins University, The Writers Center, and The George Washington University, who read drafts of the stories. Particular gratitude to Beth Greenfeld and Carol Solomon for their careful reading and rereading of these pages and for their incisive and helpful comments and suggestions.

Thanks to Anna LeBlanc for her interest in the Jewish community in Edinburgh; to Sharon Corton for sharing her scraps; to Graham Hardy, serials librarian at the Royal Botanical Gardens, Edinburgh, Scotland, for guiding the planting of Addy's garden; to Marianne Smith and Steven Kerr at the Royal College of Surgeons for information about the medical school calendar and curriculum; to Harvey Kaplan for information about Jewish cemeteries in Edinburgh in the

1920s; to R. Mitchell at the National Library of Scotland for information about newspapers read in Edinburgh in the 1930s; to Mark Norton for photographs of Birmingham in the 1950s; to Philip Ward, community relations librarian for the city of Sydney, for information about *The Sydney Morning Herald*; to Shirley Bateman, reader development and library team leader at the Southbank Library in Melbourne, for information about the publication of *A Town Like Alice*; and to Suzanne Bardgett, head of research at the Imperial War Museums, for information about reserved occupations.

Finally, thanks to my family, Tim, Jen, Fran, Aley, and Maya, for the joy they bring to my life, and to Andy, whose love makes everything possible.

Made in the
USA
Columbia, SC